THE COWGIRL'S LITTLE SECRET

SILVER JAMES

D0036200

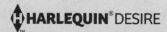

HARLEQUIN® DESIRE

Recycling programs
for this product may
not exist in your area.

ISBN-13: 978-0-373-73381-1

The Cowgirl's Little Secret

Copyright © 2015 by Silver James

Printed in U.S.A.

www.Harlequin.com

Cord settled the child he was pretty damn sure was his son more firmly on his lap.

"Is he mine?" He was pleased his voice remained calm and sounded reasonable. Inside he was a seething cauldron of anger.

CJ stopped squirming, as if he sensed something momentous about to happen. His eyes jittered between his mom and Cord.

"I..." Jolie looked away. "Cord...you don't understand."

"No. I guess I don't. Since you didn't give me a chance. Or explain. But you didn't answer my question. He is mine, isn't he?"

Anger swirled, cramping his gut. His eyes stayed fixed on Jolie, and even though they burned, he didn't blink. How could she do this to him? Did she hate him that damned much?

When he'd caught her crying over him in the hospital, he'd hoped for a second chance, but she'd obviously wiped the slate clean and eradicated him completely. His heart turned to granite when he realized what Jolie had done—and had done deliberately. If he said a word, his face would crack, shattering just like his heart was doing. But he had to know.

"Were you ever going to tell me?"

* * *

The Cowgirl's Little Secret
is part of the Red Dirt Royalty series: These Oklahoma millionaires work hard and play harder.

* * *

If you're on Twitter,
tell us what you think of Harlequin Desire!
#harlequindesire

Dear Reader,

I was at a writer's retreat presenting a workshop on creativity and one of the questions I asked the participants was, "What if...?" As an author, it's one of my favorite "games." Red Dirt Royalty began with "What if there is a powerful Oklahoma family that pretty much runs everything?" And so five brothers came to life. Cordell Barron appeared in the first Red Dirt Royalty book, *Cowgirls Don't Cry*, as his younger brother's conscience and devil's advocate. He's fun, a bit of a flirt, and no one would know he'd suffered a broken heart. So I asked myself, what if that long-ago love returned? And what if she had a big ol' honkin' secret guaranteed to break Cord's heart all over again? Would there be any way for the two of them to rediscover the love they once shared?

Those are the questions I set out to answer in this book. You see, I knew Cord needed his own story as soon as he appeared on the page in the first book. And he deserved a heroine who would run him ragged. Jolene Davis definitely does that, plus she's the daughter of oil magnate J. Rand Davis, a business rival of the Barrons.

Getting Cord and Jolie together for their second chance at love was fun for me to write, and I hope it is just as fun to read for you. I love hearing from readers, so please let me know how you feel about the Barron boys.

Happy reading,

Silver James

Silver James likes walks on the wild side, and coffee. Okay. She *loves* coffee. Warning: her muse, Iffy, runs with scissors. A cowgirl at heart, she's also been an army officer's wife and mom and has worked in the legal field, fire service and law enforcement. Now retired from the real world, she lives in Oklahoma and spends her days writing with the assistance of her two Newfoundland dogs, the cat who rules them all and the myriad characters living in her imagination. She loves interacting with readers on her blog, Twitter and Facebook. Find her at silverjames.com.

Books by Silver James

HARLEQUIN DESIRE

Red Dirt Royalty

Cowgirls Don't Cry
The Cowgirl's Little Secret

To my family and friends for not laughing when I talk out loud to the characters living in my head. To my readers, who bring joy and enthusiasm into my world and keep me at the keyboard day in and day out. To the fantastic Harlequin folks who give great edits, support and covers. All y'all are the best!

One

Cordell Barron was always in control—of his life, Barron Oil and Gas Exploration, everything that made up his world. Except for now. At the moment, Cord's world was crashing down around his ears and his life seemed to be spinning out of control.

He stared at his hands, curled so tightly around the steering wheel that his knuckles were white. *Jolie is home. Stay away from her.* The words, spoken just over a month ago by her father, were seared into Cord's memory. Like the woman.

Jolene Davis. Juliet to his Romeo—right down to their feuding families. Cord had walked away from her, not once but twice, if their hookup for "old time's sake" five years ago counted. Technically, she'd walked away the second time—before he could. Turnabout was fair play and all that crap. That was what he'd told himself at the time. He hadn't wanted to admit how much it hurt—waking up hungover to find her gone, the sheets still smelling of her sweet mimosa scent. Even now, all these years later, he hated spring when the mimosa trees bloomed.

Jerking his thoughts back to the present, he stared out the windshield of his crew-cab pickup. His fingers drummed a nervous tattoo on the console. He should call his brother Cash. Technically, they were half brothers, but Cord was head of Barron Security. He could find out everything about Jolie in an hour. Her phone number. Where she lived. Worked. Boyfriend's name. His heart thudded at the thought she might have one—or worse, a husband. He pounded the heel of his fist on the console, making his phone jump onto the passenger seat. Cord had no right to dictate anything about Jolie's life, but the thought of her in another man's arms, accepting his kisses, sharing his bed…

What was wrong with him? He was supposedly the easy-going Barron, the good ole boy comedian. He didn't get angry. He didn't slam his fist into inanimate objects— especially when it would hurt like hell. Except when Jolie was around. He was always off balance where she was concerned, like a pinball game with lights flashing and bells clanging as a huge TILT strobed in front of his eyes. Yeah, that definitely summed up their relationship. They'd been headed for a big, fat game over from the moment he first laid eyes on her.

The tune of "Take This Job and Shove It" rang out from his phone, sending him scrambling to retrieve it. He un-clenched his fist and answered with a terse "What?"

"Hey, cuz, catch you at a bad time?"

Cord clamped down on his emotions, shifting into busi-ness mode to talk to his cousin Cooper Tate, operations manager of BarEx, the Barrons' energy company. "Funny, Coop."

"Just as I suspected, we lost the drill bit down the hole." Annoyance and something akin to chagrin colored Coo-per's voice. "The crew has to fish it out. You gonna get outta the truck and come up or what?"

Glaring through the windshield at the group of men standing around on the floor of the drilling rig, Cord re-plied, "Or what, smart-ass?"

"Will you just get your butt up here? We need to talk."

A wicked dust devil of red dirt kicked up and spun across the bare expanse of the well site. Rather than cool-ing the air, the wind seared everything in its path like a blast from a furnace. The block and tackle attached to the crown of the derrick creaked and swung in a desultory arc, and a length of drilling pipe gripped in the hoist tongs swayed with a gust.

Inured to the hot August weather, Cord shoved his phone into the hip pocket of his jeans, snagged his hard hat from the passenger seat and climbed out of the white truck bearing the BarEx emblem on its doors. The metal steps leading from the ground to the drilling floor rang beneath Cord's boots. Heat waves shimmering around him, Cord gripped the steel handrail during a quick flash of vertigo. His hand felt scorched as he released the rail and climbed again.

On the rig floor, Cooper introduced him to the tool pusher. "Cord, Tom Bradley, best damn rig manager we have."

Cord shook hands with the older man, who then turned to spit tobacco juice before saying, "Damn rig sure seems to be jinxed, boss. Y'all think there's somethin' to the problems we've been having?"

Taking off his hard hat for a moment to brush fingers through his hair, Cooper finally spoke. "I… Maybe. Too many injuries. Too many delays. We should be down to oil sand by now but we aren't even close. Seems as if something happens every other day."

His cousin took a long, controlled breath. Coop was rock solid, and if he was nervous about the situation, then something was definitely wrong. Cord waited for the other man to continue.

"Remember how much trouble we had acquiring the rights to drill this one?"

"Yeah." Cord didn't like where Cooper was probably headed.

"We had a helluva bidding war with Davis Petroleum." Coop inhaled again. "Do you think they might be behind our troubles?"

His gut cramped. Coop had gone right where Cord suspected. J. Rand Davis was a rabid competitor. The man had a habit of interfering in Barron family business. Not to mention he was Jolie's father.

"No," Cord replied after some consideration. "I don't think so. Ah, hell, Cooper. I have no frickin' idea if the man would stoop that low or not." He swallowed the flood of saliva in his mouth and jerked his cousin a few steps away. Lowering his voice, he said, "Jolie's back."

Not everyone in the family knew about the fiasco that had been Cord and Jolie in college. That drunken night when, as a senior at the University of Oklahoma, Cord had run into her at a fraternity party and the bright-eyed freshman, well on her way to a massive hangover, had fallen into his lap, kissed him and cussed him out for never asking her out in high school. Learning she'd wanted him like he'd wanted her had felt like a kick in the gut from a twelve-hundred-pound Brahman bull.

But Cooper was Cord's age, a fraternity brother and friend. He'd covered for them when Cord couldn't stay away from the daughter of his father's biggest rival. And Coop had been the one to act as designated driver the night Cord had broken up with Jolie because his father, Cyrus Barron, had dictated that his second son walk away from the one girl he'd ever loved. Coward that he was, Cord had done as his father decreed and then proceeded to get and stay drunk for a week.

"Ah, hell, cuz. That sucks."

And didn't that just sum it up in a nutshell. "Yeah. It does."

Coop turned back to the tool pusher. Tuning out the continuing discussion, Cord studied the rig with a practiced eye. The workers stood around in groups, hands shoved into jeans' pockets, hard hats pushed back on their heads, clothes covered in drilling mud and grease while they waited for orders. The derrick hand was camped out on the monkey board—the platform at the top of the derrick. His job at the moment was to trip pipe—adding or subtracting lengths during the drilling process. Cord recognized the guy and waved, getting a yell in response.

"Yo, big boss! Let's get the damn bit fished out so we can get back to work."

The man had a point. More talk wouldn't get the rig back to drilling for oil. Cord turned to the knot of men still arguing outside the doghouse.

"Billy's right. We have to get that bit out before we can do anything."

At Cord's order, the crew snapped to work. The heavy, burned-oil smell of diesel mixed with the chemical tang of drilling mud. Cord grinned. He felt alive out here on the rig. These guys were real. Hard men in a hard industry. He'd started as a roughneck, back in college, learning the business literally from the ground up. If things had been different, he could have happily worked the oil patch and not missed the Barron lifestyle.

Maybe.

He returned to the mind space he alternately avoided and spent way too much time in lately—thoughts of Jolie. Back when they were younger, he'd been short of options. Stay with her and fight to work in his chosen profession or say goodbye and have his career guaranteed and filled with perks. His father had threatened that Cord would never work in the oil business if he disobeyed him. And as kids, the Barron boys knew their old man didn't make empty threats. No rival company would hire him, according to his father, and he'd believed it. In hindsight, things might have been different, but he'd been too immature and spoiled at the time to test his father's decree.

With the workers settling into a well-rehearsed routine, Cord turned to enter the doghouse. A panicked shout halted him in his tracks.

He spun around and swore time warped into slow motion.

A chain snapped from the stand of pipe just above the

drilling hole. One end whipped out, catching one of the roughnecks across his chest. The man fell to the deck as his coworkers ducked. A section of pipe swung wildly from the tongs at the top of the derrick. Up on the monkey board, Billy scrambled to control the block and tackle. Men scattered amid the grinding clash of steel on iron and the wet smack of metal meeting flesh.

Cord tracked the arcs of both the chain and the falling pipe. Cooper stood squarely in the path of both. Acting completely on instinct, Cord lunged toward his cousin. Shoulder lowered like a linebacker, he caught Coop in the middle of the back, toppling the other man off the edge of the drilling floor. Arms flailing, Cooper hit the dirt twenty feet below. Cord had no time for regrets or to worry about how bad Cooper was hurt. The loose pipe crashed into his back, driving him to his knees, where the end of the flailing chain clipped him around the top of his rib cage. As his head smacked the steel flooring, he had time for one thought before succumbing to darkness.

Damn. This is gonna hurt when I wake up.

Jolie Davis stared at the empty whiteboard filling an entire wall of the intake section of University Hospital's Trauma One. She was bored out of her skull. And she was pulling a double shift.

When she moved back to Oklahoma City, she'd planned to get out of the ER, but then University had offered her a big salary and a humongous sign-on bonus. She'd jumped at the opportunity to prove to her dad she could take care of herself. And CJ. It was bad enough her father had bought her a house and hired a nanny. He'd take over her entire life if she didn't fight him every inch of the way. That was his modus operandi. The man was a type A personality and she was his only child, which made CJ his only grandson. To say J. Rand Davis was a little overprotective was like calling the Grand Canyon a ditch.

Midweek was a slow time for the ER. Usually. But this was Oklahoma. A late-season thunderstorm could blow up and wreak havoc. Or there could be a big wreck on one of the major interstates crisscrossing the Oklahoma City metroplex. Tinker Air Force Base and Will Rogers World Airport meant airplanes. Lots of them. They could… Not that she really wished ill on anyone, but when things were slow, she had way too much time to think.

Every time the front doors slithered open, she could see the monolithic Barron Tower arrowing up into the hot blue Oklahoma sky. Cord's office was there. No. She would *not* think about him. That part of her life was over. She was better off without him.

The thought squeezed her chest as tight as Scarlett O'Hara's corset. Jolie remembered to inhale when white dots sparkled in her vision. Thoughts of Cord always did this to her. Everyone told her to live her life. How sad was it she only wanted to live that life with him? Despite everything. Because of everything. But there was a zero percent chance of that happening. The imaginary corset cinched even tighter as guilt washed over her. He'd never forgive her for what she'd done.

Jolie rolled her head from shoulder to shoulder, and then stretched. Maybe she'd go wash the empty whiteboard. Again. Whirling the desk chair around, her legs collided with a smiling man. Dr. Perry, attending surgeon on duty and head of Trauma One. She squeaked, her heart pounding. "Dang! Don't sneak up on me like that."

Absently rubbing his knee where she'd banged the chair into him, Dr. Perry chuckled. "I didn't think I was. I'm headed to the cafeteria. Want me to bring you something back? You know what it's like in the ER. We eat when we—" The doctor tilted his head as if listening to something she couldn't hear.

Sirens. So much for a quiet afternoon. She did her best to hide her elation at being busy.

After a couple hours, things had settled back down. A med tech had his hip propped on Jolie's desk and was teasing her while she sipped the mocha frappuccino he'd brought to bribe her to go out with him.

"Do you like kids?" She knew how to nip his interest in the bud.

"They're cute in the petting zoo."

Jolie rolled her eyes. "I'm not talking about baby goats."

"Neither am I." His eyes twinkled, though he managed to keep a straight face. The theme song from *Pirates of the Caribbean* filled the air and he dug his cell phone out of his scrubs. With a wave and a wink, he disappeared around the corner.

Leaning back in her chair, Jolie exhaled. So far, they'd dealt with a suspect bitten by a police dog, a teenage girl who'd twisted her ankle during a fast-pitch softball game and a guy who'd tried to amputate his thumb with a chain saw. The cops had flirted with her, the softball player's parents had been upset the girl might miss the rest of the tournament and Chain Saw Guy's wife had yelled at him for being stupid. Jolie sort of had to agree with that assessment.

Just then, the statewide emergency network radio squawked. Dr. Perry appeared out of nowhere and snagged the microphone before she could. He acknowledged the call and put it on loudspeaker without missing a beat. Jolie took triage notes while he questioned the EMT on the other end.

An accident on a drilling rig. Three patients. The most critical would be arriving by the MedFlight helicopter currently being dispatched. Jolie activated a second chopper to bring in the second patient, a man who'd fallen twenty feet.

Trauma One looked like an anthill that had been kicked. Scurrying people appeared from nowhere, everyone intent on preparing the ER. Jolie kept track of the trauma clock— the indefinable golden hour providing the best odds for full recovery.

The electronic exit doors whooshed open and closed but

she heard it—the *whap-whap-whap* of helicopter blades. The radio crackled. She breathed—and it seemed as if Trauma One breathed with her as the pilot's voice ghosted from the speaker.

"MedFlight One to base."

She cleared her throat before keying the microphone. "This is base. Go ahead, Med One." Jolie wrote on the whiteboard as the flight nurse gave her the rundown on the patient's life-threatening injuries while the chopper landed.

"Roger that, Med One."

Medical personnel scrambled to the helipad, returning quickly with the first victim. As Jolie fell into step beside the gurney, she glanced over and saw the patient's face. Then faltered and tripped. One of the interns bumped into her, but kept her from going down with a steadying hand under her elbow. She murmured apologies and trotted to catch up.

This wasn't happening. That was *not* Cordell Barron on that gurney. *Oh, God, it couldn't be.*

Two

Instinct kept her making notes as her conscious brain froze. One word kept screaming through her mind. *No. No, no, no, no, no* turned into a litany. This was so wrong. Things weren't supposed to end this way.

The flight nurse passed Cord's driver's license to her and Jolie accepted it with numb fingers. "Patient's ID says his name is Cordell Barron. Thirty-three years old. Wonder if he's one of *the* Barrons?"

Jolie nodded mutely. Oh, yeah. Cord was definitely one of them. Her fingers shook as she tried to type in information on the computer pad.

The gurney was wheeled into the trauma bay but she stopped at the edge of the curtain. She had to call his next of kin. It was her job. That would be his father. Cyrus Barron. The man who'd ruined her life. She couldn't do it, couldn't speak to that man for her life. Or Cord's.

The steady beeping of the monitors switched to a sharp alarm. He was crashing. Jolie forgot everything but saving the life of the only man she'd ever loved. Reflexes honed by five years working trauma kicked in. She passed off the pad to another nurse, pulled on latex gloves and waded into the mix.

Thirty nerve-wracking minutes later, Dr. Perry and the trauma surgical team finally stabilized Cord and whisked him off to the operating room. Jolie watched the elevator doors close behind the gurney before she turned back to the ER bay where they'd worked so feverishly to save his life. Her knees wobbled, and she had to lean against the wall to stay upright. Her night wasn't over yet. Cooper Tate was still being worked on by the orthopedic team, his compound fractures serious though not life threatening. He'd be following Cord into surgery shortly.

Trauma One looked as if a tornado had torn through it. Jolie went through the robotic motions of cleaning up and resetting the bay for the third patient coming in by ambulance from the well site. She should be back at the admitting desk filling out the paperwork on Cord and Cooper. Should be notifying their families. The clothes Cord had been wearing, along with his personal effects, had been shoved into a plastic bin for safekeeping. She tucked the tub under her arm and shuffled back to the intake desk as the janitorial staff moved in to mop and sanitize.

Sinking into her chair, Jolie felt as if she'd just run a marathon—her arms and legs were leaden, her brain still in shock. Shivering uncontrollably, she wrapped her arms across her chest and hung on, breathing deeply until the worst of the reaction passed. There wasn't time to collapse. Not yet. She had to make notifications. No matter what. It was her job as admitting nurse. She couldn't pass it off—no matter how much she wanted to do so. Bad enough she'd all but abandoned her post to work on Cord.

The bin with Cord's belongings sat at her feet. She bent over and dug through the ripped and bloody clothes. She flipped open his wallet. Credit cards. A couple of receipts. No list of contact phone numbers. Jolie tucked the wallet and his driver's license into a plastic baggy. She did not stare at his photo. She didn't sigh over those sculpted cheekbones and that strong jaw, the golden-brown eyes. She didn't rub her thumb across the plastic pretending it was his face and she could feel his skin. Well, just once. Or twice.

Something dinged. Startled, Jolie dropped the ID and grabbed her cell phone. Its face remained dark. The strains of something country and western played from deep in the bin. She found Cord's phone in the hip pocket of his jeans. The caller ID read Cash.

Knowing she should answer, Jolie let it roll to voice mail. Cash didn't like her. Truth be told, none of Cord's brothers liked her. Well, except maybe for Chance. While he might not *like* her, he didn't hate her like the rest of the family. Chance and Cooper. They'd been the only ones to ever give her the time of day when she'd dated Cord.

Cord's phone was password protected. Of course it was, because nothing could be easy tonight. She stared off into the distance, thinking. She tried his birth date. Nope. On a whim, she tried her own. That had been his default password for everything when they dated in college. When the screen opened, she almost dropped the phone. Jolie scrolled through his contact list, making note of pertinent numbers for the hospital's records. She had to stop dithering and make at least one call. Chance's number was at the top of the list. She dialed it on her desk phone but remembered Chance was on his honeymoon, so she hung up.

Jolie remembered the big dust up from early in the summer as she had been moving home. Seemed as if Cyrus Barron was still screwing up his sons' lives—Chance's this time. The woman he'd fallen for had led an old-fashioned cattle drive from her ranch to the stockyards to get her steers to market so she could pay off the mortgage lien Cyrus held on the place. She knew how Mr. Barron reacted to his sons thinking for themselves. He wouldn't like it one little bit, especially if Chance went against his father's dictates, siding with a woman Cyrus had declared an enemy. Jolie had heard all about that day because her dad had been waiting on Cassie Morgan to arrive so he could buy the herd. Yeah, her dad liked screwing with the Barron family.

Worrying her bottom lip with her teeth, Jolie stared at the phone numbers on her list. Chance and Cord were close, with Cooper their third musketeer. As soon as Chance

heard the news, he'd be on the next plane home anyway—
honeymoon or not. Decision made, Jolie used Cord's phone
to call.

After six rings, she was afraid her call would roll over
to voice mail. Chance picked up on the eighth ring.

"Dude, this better be important." His voice held a teasing growl.

Using her most professional voice, Jolie said, "This is
University Hospital Trauma One calling. Mr. Chance Barron?"

"What the— How? What the hell's going on?"

"I'm sorry to inform you, sir, but your brother Cord was
critically injured. An accident on an oil rig."

"Is he… How bad?"

"He's—" Her voice cracked and she had to swallow
around the constriction in her throat. "He's in surgery,
Cha—Mr. Barron."

She almost blew it, calling him by his first name. After
giving him all the information she had, she heard Chance's
barely polite goodbye before he hung up on her. Jolie hud-
dled her shoulders, shaking again. What if Cord died?

The 11:00 p.m. shift change arrived. Jolie was dead on
her feet and emotionally drained. She'd finished her double
shift in automatic mode. Standing in the humid air outside
the ER, she stared in the direction of the parking garage.
She should go home, take a long bubble bath and put everything behind her. But she couldn't.

Cord Barron had almost died today. Her stomach
cramped so hard she had to bend over from the waist. Jolie
choked back a whimper. She wanted to hate him. Had tried
to hate him. She'd been the one wanting to kill him—with
air quotes around that sentiment. *Kill 'im dead.* Every day
since he'd walked out without a word. No goodbye. No explanation. Nothing. Until she had seen him sitting at the
bar in Hannigan's that long ago St. Paddy's Day. She'd rec-

ognized the hungry look in his eyes and the bulge in his jeans. And something had snapped. She'd wanted to hurt him as badly as he'd hurt her.

Oh, yeah. She'd really taught him a lesson that night—spending the night and then slipping out of the penthouse hotel room at dawn. Only she was the one with the constant reminder. Every time she looked into her son's eyes and he smiled, Cord was right there all over again.

Rubbing her temples, she breathed deeply to hold back nausea. Jolie didn't head to the parking garage. She pivoted on her heel and headed back inside the hospital. Marching to the elevator, she berated herself for her weakness with each step until it became a mantra.

This is a bad idea. A really bad idea.

Cord was out of surgery, but she had to see for herself. She needed to make sure his injuries weren't as life threatening as they'd looked when he'd stopped breathing in the ER.

Pushing through the double doors of the ICU ward, Jolie passed her hand under the automatic dispenser for hand sanitizer from force of habit. The hushed whoosh and thump of respiratory machines were a soft counterpoint to the electronic beeps of heart monitors. Bright lights kept shadows confined to corners. Life and death battled here, with medical personnel on the front lines.

She glanced at the board to locate Cord's room number. Determined to just stick her head in to assess his condition and leave, Jolie parted the curtains of his cubicle. He looked drawn and pale amid the snaking mass of wires and tubes. She glanced at the monitor, judged his heart rate, respirations and blood pressure.

A touch on her shoulder caused Jolie to clap her hand over her mouth to contain a startled scream. The charge nurse offered a crooked smile.

"What brings you up here, Jolie?"

Jolie nodded toward the bed. "He's a…" A what? Friend?

Lover? Ex? More? Definitely less at this point in time. "I know him." That was a generic-enough response. "I was in the ER when he was brought in. I just wanted to check on him before I head home."

The nurse studied her for a long silent minute, and then her expression softened with something akin to understanding. "Sure, hon. Take your time."

When the nurse stepped away and ducked into another room, Jolie logged into the computer station outside Cord's room and checked his chart. Things were serious but he was no longer at death's door.

She should go home, but the thought of the empty house waiting for her didn't appeal. CJ was staying with his grandfather and Mrs. Corcoran, the nanny, was off visiting her sister. Without giving her motives too much thought, she pulled up an uncomfortable-looking chair and sank gratefully into it. She'd never get this opportunity again—the chance to study Cord, to hold his hand, to pretend what might have been. Jolie curled her fingers around his and simply devoured him with her gaze.

Dark hair hung over the bandage circling his head. He still wore it shaggy, though one side had been shaved for the stitches needed to close the gash on his head. More bandages covered his abdomen, and a wound vac clicked with each draining suck. Though his eyes were closed, she knew they were the color of burned honey. His face was sculpted into stark planes. A dark shadow covered his cheeks and chin. Though bristly now, the stubble would be soft by morning. The fingers of her free hand curled and flexed with the effort not to stroke him.

Cord's bare chest—what she could see of it—and his shoulders had the raw look of a man who worked for a living. He'd always been buff. In high school, it was sports and summers working on the Crown B Ranch. In college, he worked the oil patch, getting a hands-on education supplemented by his classroom studies.

A wide yawn cracked her jaw. She glanced at the wall clock, surprised it was almost 2:00 a.m. She started to pull her hand away, but Cord's fingers tightened on hers and his eyelids fluttered. Thrilled, her heart and lungs performed *Riverdance*, but she didn't want to examine his reaction too closely, choosing to pretend it heralded a change for the better in his condition. Not something else. As if he knew it was her.

"Don't go."

His voice rasped across her nerves and Jolie could no longer hide from her feelings. His grip tightened around her fingers, and his respirations and heart rate kicked off alarms on the monitor.

"Please."

Tears burned behind her eyelids. "Okay."

Her whispered assurance eased him, evidenced by the way the monitor sounds evened out. One corner of his mouth quirked into a faint semblance of the cocky grin she'd once loved so much.

"Okay." Darkness dragged him under again.

The sweet summer scent of mimosa filled Cord with a sense of rightness. Jolie. Jolie always smelled like mimosa. He cracked one eye open, ignoring the obnoxious sounds of his hospital room and the pain. He inhaled again but that sweet aroma was overwhelmed by the stench of antiseptic and alcohol, of sickness and death. Walls painted institutional gray surrounded him but he found his balance. Jolie. Here? He was too groggy to wonder about the how or why of it.

Slumped over, her head resting on the bed, Jolie held his hand. She puffed air softly in her sleep as a sunbeam kissed her cheek. He hadn't dreamed her. She *was* here. Touching him. He ached to touch her chestnut hair but knew any movement would do two things: hurt like hell and startle her into letting go. Instead, he remained content to simply be with her. He'd wanted her and here she was. Sleeping in a position guaranteeing a trip to a chiropractor, holding his hand and making those cute breathing noises he still dreamed about.

Five years ago, during their brief and disastrous reunion, despite the fact both of them had had far too much to drink, he'd made love to her and she'd fallen asleep in his arms. He craved the feeling again like an addict falling out of a twelve-step program. He could admit, at least to himself, that he'd loved her since high school. Not that it did him— or her—any good. Jolie was a Davis, her father a rival of his. And Cyrus Barron always made damn sure Cord and his brothers played by his rules. He hated his old man.

A commotion out in the ward ratcheted the noise level up a notch. Speak of the devil himself. Cord slitted his eyelids. Maybe his father would go away if he thought he was still unconscious.

"What the hell is she doing here?" Cyrus Barron bellowed as he entered the room, and would have lunged for the bed if not for Cash restraining him.

Jolie jerked awake, her heart pounding from the adrenaline rush. Glancing around in an attempt to focus her sleep-fuzzy mind, she remembered. She'd fallen asleep at Cord's bedside.

The supervising nurse followed Mr. Barron and Cash into the small room. "Keep your voice down, sir, or I'll ask you to leave."

Cyrus, red in the face and looking ready for battle, opened his mouth to launch into what promised to be a scathing retort. Cash cut him off.

"Enough, Dad. Cord's still unconscious. We don't want to disturb him."

Lowering his voice, Cyrus issued orders. "Get her out of here. That woman is not to be anywhere near my son. Especially not with her head on his damn bed!"

Jolie bristled, but the nurse replied before she could. "Ms. Davis is doing her job, Mr. Barron. If you interfere with her or any of my personnel, I will have you not only removed right this instant but banned from this hospital." She fisted her hands on her hips. "I don't care who you are. This is my department and you will follow my rules. Or else."

Jolie rolled her lips between her teeth and bit down to hide a grin. No one but no one ever talked to Cyrus Barron that way. The man was completely flummoxed and left speechless for a moment.

"What is your name?" he demanded.

"Meg Dabney, RN." The nurse arched a brow. "I'm the day-shift supervisor." Giving Cyrus her back, she stared at Jolie. "Do you have the patient's vitals, Jolie?"

Meg was giving her an out—thank goodness. Jolie stood up and quickly assessed the monitor numbers, while twisting her hand to make it look as if she'd been taking Cord's pulse manually. She read off the statistics while the older woman made notes on her electronic pad. Jolie came close to freaking out when something tickled her palm: Cord's index finger. She peered at him and noticed his eyelids flickering. Faker! He was conscious and enjoying the show. Relief warred with irritation. This was so like the blasted man.

Dropping his hand, Jolie backed away from the bed. Head down, refusing to make eye contact with Cyrus, she slipped around Meg. The brush of a hand on her bare arm startled her and she glanced up. Cash inclined his head in a slight nod and offered a sympathetic smile, which surprised the dickens out of her. Cash hated her. Didn't he?

Before she could get away, more Barrons crowded in. Chance and a woman she recognized from the society pages as his new bride, Cassidy. Chase, the Mr. Vegas playboy brother, and even Clay, who must have come all the way from DC. All five Barron brothers in the same small space were enough to put a girl into libido overload, as evidenced by the envious looks from the other nurses.

She escaped, but not for long. Chance caught up to her in three strides.

"Jolie?"

She shoved her hands into the pockets of her rumpled scrubs and wished she'd had time to brush her teeth. With her head still down, she glanced at him from the corner of her eyes. "Hi, Chance. Uh…congratulations on your marriage. You got here quickly."

"Thanks. The joys of having a fleet of private jets on standby. Are you okay?"

That brought her head up and she met his concerned gaze. "Why wouldn't I be?"

As Cord's brother studied her, she tilted her chin and pasted a blank expression on her face.

"How is he, really?"

She'd bet this was not the real question on the tip of his tongue, but Chance had a reputation as one of the best courtroom attorneys in the state. She lifted one shoulder in a negligent shrug. "Far better than he has a right to be."

Chance's eyes narrowed and a frown tugged at the corners of his mouth. Realizing how that sounded, Jolie hastened to explain.

"He almost died, Chance. And probably should have." A shiver skittered through her. "He coded in the ER last night, but he's strong. And stubborn." And far too aware of her presence this morning, damn him. "The doctors are worried about the liver tear and the spinal injury."

"What about the trauma to his head?"

She choked on an involuntary giggle. "As thick as his skull is?" She sobered and exhaled. "He'll recover fully from the concussion. The scar will be hidden once his hair grows back out."

Disconcerted by Chance's continued scrutiny, she turned away. "I have to go."

He gripped her shoulder gently, halting her in her tracks. "Thank you, Jolie. Thank you for being here for him, for not leaving him alone. And for calling me."

She twisted her head around to stare at him. While not as big a playboy as Chase, Chance had been a player and rather shallow, except where his brothers were concerned. The Barron boys were nothing if not absolutely loyal to each other. She glanced toward the blonde, who stood in the doorway of Cord's room watching them. Cassidy Morgan had changed Chance Barron for the better.

Jolie glanced back into the cubicle where Cord was still faking unconsciousness. Too bad he appeared to be the same old Cord.

Three

Jolie tiptoed past the ICU waiting room. Even after a week and at five in the morning, at least one Barron family member was camped out there. She shouldn't be here. Had no right to slip into his room to check his chart, to stare at him, to miss him so much she couldn't breathe sometimes.

Cordell Barron was the man she loved to hate. And hated to love. But love him she did, God help her. She remembered the first time she'd seen him as vividly as if it had happened yesterday. Her first day of high school. Standing at the top of the stairs, she'd glimpsed the guys all the freshmen girls were talking about. The Barron brothers. Cord. Chance. And their cousins, Cooper and Boone Tate.

Rooted to the spot, she'd gazed down at him. He'd looked up and snagged her with his gaze. That maddening smile of his had slid across his face and broadened until dimples appeared to bracket his full lips. Love at first sight. But then Boone had said something and Cord's expression had sharpened before they'd all turned and walked away. She should have seen the truth even then. That was only the first time he'd walked away from her.

As she parted the curtains of his room, the sight of him kicked her in the chest just like that first time. Unshed tears prickled the back of her nose and her throat burned. Her fingers itched to comb his thick hair off his forehead before tangling in the dark silk of it. Why did she come every morning? This was torture. Things hadn't changed. His father still hated her, still pulled all the strings. And it wasn't just herself she had to worry about now. There was CJ, too.

"You just gonna stand there or are you gonna come in and say hello?" Cord's raspy voice raised goose bumps on her arms.

"I didn't mean to wake you."

"C'mere."

"No. I mean…I have to go. My shift starts soon."

"Jolie. Please."

Oh, God, how could she ignore the pleading in those beautiful burned-honey eyes of his? Dragging her feet, she approached the bed and stood at its foot. His gaze raked over her, hot and hungry, and…yes, there was the hurt she expected to see. Well, good. Now they were even.

"Thank you."

She blinked as her jaw dropped a little. Those were not the words she'd expected to fall out of his mouth. "F-for what?"

"For being in the ER. For calling Chance. For staying with me."

"You remember?"

"Yeah. I'm sorry my old man is such an asshat." He offered a crooked grin that indented only one cheek with a dimple as he held out the hand not plugged full of needles and tubes. "C'mere, Jolie."

Her fingers curled and her hand started to reach for him of its own accord. She smoothed her palm against her scrub pants and forced her fingers to grab the cotton instead of his warm flesh. "I can't, Cord. You know that. I have to go." She turned to leave but his voice stopped her, the plaintive tone twisting her heart.

"Jolie?"

She listened to him inhale and her shoulders slumped. He sounded so…defeated. Glancing over her shoulder, she forced her feet to remain planted. Everything in her wanted to run to him, to wrap him in her arms. The pain—physical and emotional—on his face almost undid her.

"I...I can't, Cord. We can't." She fled, dashing tears from her eyes as she pushed through the ICU doors only to smack into a very solid chest. Strong arms gripped her biceps, holding her up.

"Jolie? You okay?"

Chance. Just her luck.

The timbre of his voice changed. "Jolie? Is it Cord? Is he okay? Did something happen?"

Oh, yeah. Something happened. She'd fallen in love with a man she couldn't have, she'd seduced him to get back at him, and then she'd kept a big ole honkin' secret from him. One that would make him hate her. Breathing deeply to steady her nerves, she blinked away the tears.

"He's awake, Chance. You can talk to him. I have to go. I'm on shift in a few minutes." She tried to step around him but he didn't release her.

"He still loves you, Jolie."

Her heart ripped just a little more. "No, he doesn't. If he loved me, he would have never broken my...broken up with me."

She jerked free and stalked away. She kept her head up and shoulders stiff even though she wanted to hunch over to contain the pain ripping her apart.

Jolie didn't come back. Cord was disappointed. And pissed. Was she just teasing him again? Anger washed over him like a big ocean wave, filling him with enough bitterness to choke him. One week rolled over into two weeks, and then the third one dragged by with no sign of her. Fine. He was stupid to think they might have a chance, that she'd visited because she still cared.

He fidgeted, waiting for the doctor to arrive. After a month in the hospital, rumor had it he might be discharged today. He was more than ready to get out. To get away from any reminder of Jolie. She was just a few floors away, down in Trauma One. He'd caught a glimpse of her once, as a physical therapist had wheeled him past the cafeteria. She'd taken one look at him in the wheelchair, blanched, turned and all but ran away.

Yeah. He knew the feeling. He hated the freaking chair. Hated that his legs still didn't work quite right, that his head felt like a watermelon splattered on hot pavement whenever he looked into a bright light, that he was crippled. Cord wanted to go home, where he no longer had to see pity on the faces surrounding him.

Chance and Cassie arrived, followed closely by the doctor and his entourage of medical students. Ah, the joys of University being a teaching hospital. *Not.*

Seeing his state of undress, his sister-in-law immediately split, offering to grab coffee from the waiting room. Cord would be damned glad when he could wear clothes again so his dangly bits didn't offend anyone.

He put up with the poking, prodding, comments and advice. The doctor used a stylus to record stuff on a touch screen tablet, frowning as he filled in blanks. Cord's heart sank. He was going to be stuck here even longer.

"Meg will bring all the paperwork and go over your therapy plan, Mr. Barron." The doctor glanced at Chance. "You've arranged for a home health aide?"

"Wait," Cord interrupted. "Does this mean I'm getting out of here?"

"That's what it means, Mr. Barron."

"Hot damn. Chance, you better have brought me a pair of pants!"

It took three hours to get out of there. Three freaking hours to clear up all the paperwork, but Cord was finally free. Sort of. He was still stuck in the wheelchair. But he wore real clothes—jeans, boots, a T-shirt that hung a little loose on him. He'd lost weight and muscle tone in the hospital, despite the burgers, fries and pizza his brothers had sneaked in and all the physical therapy exercises. But he could go home now. Get away from the hospital, where he wondered every day if he might catch a glimpse of Jolie, wanting her to come back to see him, needing it as much as a man needed water in the desert. That was how he felt. Parched. He wanted to drink her in, knew he could drown in her presence.

Chance insisted on pushing the wheelchair while Cassie carried the bags of medical supplies, paraphernalia and other stuff he'd accumulated. They rode the elevator down to the first floor in silence. Cassie waited with him while Chance went to get his truck. Once he was settled in the front passenger seat and they were underway, Chance glanced at him.

His brother cleared his throat before saying, "I thought we'd take you to the ranch."

As much as he wanted to go home to his condo and hide from the whole world, Chance's suggestion made sense. They had staff at the home place, the Crown B Ranch. Miz Beth and Big John, the caretakers who'd been with the boys for as long as they could remember. And according to the doctor, a home health aide. Cord hated being an invalid. But he'd have the place to himself. The old man, when he was in town, kept an apartment in Barron Towers. His brothers all had their own places. Only staff and Kaden Waite, the ranch manager, would be around.

"Yeah, fine. Whatever." He swallowed the snarl and added, "But I'm starved. I want a steak before we head out there."

"Cattlemen's?"

At his nod, Chance changed lanes and made a left turn to head back toward Stockyards City and the famous steak house.

Chance found a space in the parking lot behind the historic building housing Cattlemen's Cafe. After some frustrated manipulation, Cord settled into the wheelchair. Cassie insisted Chance push and Cord grimaced.

"I can push myself. I'm not helpless."

"Of course you aren't." Cassie hastened to soothe him. "But this is your chance to make Chance your minion."

Cord still wasn't happy, but the way Cassie phrased it took the sting out of the fact that he was stuck. Not for long, though. He fully planned to be rid of the freaking wheelchair as soon as possible, if not before.

They had missed the lunch rush and were too early for the dinner crowd, so they were seated immediately.

While Cord and Chance went for the large filet, Cassie opted for prime rib. Their salads were quickly followed by their entrées, and they dug in like starving people, which Cord was. Beef, for him, was its own food group.

Their meal finished, Cassie maneuvered Cord's wheelchair through the narrow aisles between seating areas while Chance stepped ahead to handle the door. The entrance to the restaurant consisted of two sets of heavy glass double doors, their handles shaped like the horns of a longhorn steer. They'd just passed through the inner doors only to stop when the exterior doors were opened by a woman wearing scrubs, holding a little boy's hand.

Jolie.

Cord watched her eyes widen to deer-in-headlights proportions as her gaze darted between him and the child beside her.

Nobody moved until Cassie elbowed Chance and whispered, "I didn't know Cord had been married."

Her voice broke the spell and both Cord and Chance stared at her.

"He hasn't."

"I haven't."

The men answered all but simultaneously.

"Why would you think he had, Cass?" Chance muttered the question.

The kid tugged at Jolie's hand. "Ow, Mommy, leggo. You're squeezin' me too hard."

Cord stared at Jolie then the boy. Mommy? She had a son? His heart shriveled like mud under a hot August sun. She'd found someone else and married him. Had his child. He relaxed his fists and smoothed damp palms along his thighs, hoping to hide his agitation. And sitting in this damned wheelchair sure didn't help his ego.

Cassie hissed, "If that little boy isn't a Barron, then I'm deaf and blind."

All the color drained from Jolie's face. Her gaze jerked to the child beside her before returning to meet Cord's stare. She swallowed convulsively and guilt radiated from her. Cord couldn't speak for a minute as Cassie's words sank in.

"Jolie?" Her name rasped across his tongue, which felt like sandpaper.

"Cord." She blinked several times and her grip on the boy's hand tightened even more.

People knotted up behind them, wanting out. Cord pushed the chair forward, and Jolie had no place to go but backward onto the sidewalk. Chance and Cassie followed a step behind.

Brown eyes as curious as a chipmunk's stared at Cord. This time, he was the one who swallowed convulsively. "What's going on, Jolie?"

"Who're you?" The boy's lips pursed and his brows knitted together.

Tilting his head so he could watch both Jolie and the boy, Cord replied, "I'm Cord Barron. Who're you?"

"I'm CJ. Do you know my mommy?"

"I thought I did." Cord was pretty sure his voice dripped icicles. Cassie was right. Everything about the kid screamed Barron. His aggressive stance, his expression. Looking at CJ was like seeing a picture of himself as a kid.

"Cord…I…I can explain."

Jolie looked terrified as he pushed the wheelchair toward her, only to be brought up short by his brother's hand on his shoulder.

"Easy, Cord. Let me handle this."

Chance was using his lawyer voice. Rather than shaking off his hand, Cord inhaled deeply. It wouldn't do to lose his temper. Not here in the middle of the sidewalk. Was it possible CJ was his? He knew nothing about kids, or how to judge their ages, but the boy couldn't be more than four, five at the oldest. He stopped breathing for a minute. St. Patrick's Day. Five years ago. The Bricktown Street Party. Hannigan's Pub. He felt the color drain from his face and now he surged forward, jerking away from his brother.

"Why didn't you tell me?"

Jolie backed up several steps, dragging the boy with her. CJ pulled free and charged. His little fists hammered Cord's thighs as Cord jerked the chair to a stop to avoid running over the kid.

"You leave my mommy alone."

Cord picked him up, hiding the twinge of pain in his ribs, and placed him in his lap, one arm corralling the kid's legs so he couldn't kick. Oh, yeah. CJ was all Barron. He had no doubt.

"Cord? Please…"

He glanced around CJ to stare at Jolie. She had her hand raised, reaching toward her son, her eyes pleading with him. Folding the kid in his arms, he settled the child he was pretty damn sure was his son more firmly on his lap. "Is he mine?" He was pleased his voice remained calm and sounded reasonable. Inside he was a seething cauldron of anger.

CJ stopped squirming, as if he sensed something momentous about to happen. His eyes jittered between his mom and Cord.

"I…" Jolie looked away. "Cord… You don't understand."

"No. I guess I don't. Since you didn't give me a chance.

Or explain. But you didn't answer my question. He is mine, isn't he?"

Anger cramped his gut, but his touch remained gentle as he held the boy in his lap. His eyes stayed fixed on Jolie, and even though they burned, he didn't blink. How could she do this to him? Did she hate him that damned much? When he'd caught her crying over him in the ICU, he'd hoped for a second chance, but she'd obviously wiped the slate clean and eradicated him completely. His heart turned to granite when he realized what Jolie had done—and had done deliberately. If he said a word, his face would crack, shattering just like his heart was doing. But he had to know.

"Were you ever going to tell me?"

Jolie flushed and her chin rose to a stubborn angle. The anger in her green eyes flashed like emeralds lit by fire-light. "No, Cord. No, I wasn't."

Four

"Let go of my son, Cord." Jolie reached for CJ, but the boy shook her off, curling in closer to Cord's shoulder.

CJ ignored his mother and cupped his hands on Cord's cheeks. The boy pulled his head around to draw his attention.

"Do you have a little boy?"

Where the dickens had that question come from? Cord studied CJ's face, noting the similarities.

"Yeah, it seems like maybe I do."

"Oh." The kid's expression shuttered as he tucked his chin against his chest. He squirmed a little, as if to get away.

With a touch of his index finger, Cord got him to look up. None of this was CJ's fault. But he had to know. *Was* there another man in Jolie's life?

"Do you have a dad?"

"No." The boy lifted his shoulders up around his ears and shot his mother a guilty look as he whispered, "I kinda wish I did."

The kid's voice did something to Cord's chest. He remembered wishing the same thing, but his old man was always too busy. At the same time, relief washed over him. There didn't seem to be a father figure in the boy's life.

"Dads are important." He offered CJ a hesitant smile.

"Cord…" Again Chance's voice, brimming with unspoken legal advice, intruded. "We need to step back from the emotions here, talk about this someplace else."

"Like your office?"

"Or home." Chance sounded diplomatic.

Cord focused on CJ. "Have you ever met your dad?"

The kid shook his head, a little smile beginning to tweak the corner of his mouth. Then he glanced around at the serious faces of the adults, and his budding smile wilted when he fixed his attention on Jolie. "Mommy? Are you cryin'?" He squirmed to get off Cord's lap.

"Don't do this, Cord. Please. Not like this."

Cord swallowed around the fist-size lump in his throat and ignored the tears shining on Jolie's cheeks and the plea in her voice. Her anger had leached out, leaving only sadness. "There's something you should know, CJ. I'm your—"

"Cord, no!" Jolie's anger was back, and it prickled his skin like dozens of needle pricks.

"Dammit, Jolie—"

"Uh-oh. You aren't s'posed to say that word."

Cord absently rubbed CJ's back as he controlled his own anger. "Yeah. I know, bubba. I'll have to start a swear jar for when I forget and say words like that in front of you."

"A swear jar?"

"Yup. Whenever you or I say a bad word, we'll have to put money in the jar. To remind us not to say them."

CJ cut his eyes to his mom and lowered his voice to a loud whisper. "Am I gonna see you again?"

"We have to go, CJ."

Jolie stood rooted about four feet away, as if afraid to approach. Probably a good idea. Not that Cord would physically harm her. He didn't hit women. But damn if he didn't want to hurt her as badly as she'd hurt him. She'd eviscerated him, spilling his heart and guts right there on the sidewalk for everyone to see.

"No."

She blinked at his cold command and opened her mouth to argue.

"I'm his father. CJ's coming with us."

CJ whipped his head around to stare, his brow crinkled. He mouthed the word *father* but Cord mostly ignored the boy, his gaze fixed on Jolie.

"The hell you say." She bore down on him now, a tiger mama ready to rip his head off.

"Bad mommy. You aren't s'posed to say those words, either!" CJ chortled and clapped his hands, oblivious to the tension among the adults. "She has to put money in the swear jar, too, right?" He blinked, long dark lashes shadowing brown eyes so reminiscent of Cord's own. Looking shy, he gazed up. "Right? Uh…" He patted Cord's cheek again to get his attention. "Are you my daddy?"

Cord felt the word deep in his chest as CJ uttered it and something shifted—something both fierce and tender.

"Absolutely, pardner." He glared at Jolie, daring her to continue the fight.

She wasn't about to back down. "C'mon, CJ."

"But, Mommy," he whined, digging in his heels by wrapping his legs around one of Cord's legs and pulling against her grip. "I want strawberry shortcake."

"Not today. We're going home."

"You're not going anywhere, Jolie. Not until this is settled."

Her gaze whipped to meet Cord's, and then skittered away from the seething anger in his expression.

"Cord, let them go. Cassie can drop me at the office and take you home. I'll get a writ of *habeas corpus* drawn up along with a request for a paternity test and file them this afternoon."

"You wouldn't dare!" Jolie barely managed to utter her outraged words.

Chance's mouth thinned into a disapproving grimace. "Damn straight I would." He ruffled CJ's hair after Cassie glared and elbowed him. "And I'll put my dollar in the swear jar, too, bubba."

"Everyone should step back a little and take a deep

breath," Cassie urged. "And Chance is right. We need to take this someplace more private." Her hands lifted in a fluttery gesture to indicate the curious stares from people passing by.

Cord didn't care if they were being filmed for a segment on the ten o'clock news, but his sister-in-law had a point. "Yeah, good idea, Cass."

Chance glanced at Cassie. "Darlin', would you get them to pack up a strawberry shortcake to go?" He winked at CJ as Cass ducked back inside the restaurant. "Are you sure we can't move this to my office?"

Jolie bowed up like a half-broke mustang, and Cord worked to school his expression. She always did run toward hot tempered.

"And give you Barrons home court advantage? I don't think so. I'll tell ya what. Let's go to my dad's office. We can talk there." She folded her arms just under her breasts, plumping them under the misshapen scrubs she wore.

Cord sucked in a breath. This woman had always had power over him. From the first moment he'd laid eyes on her standing at the top of the stairs in high school.

"I don't care where the he—" He glanced down at CJ and bit off the word. "The *heck* we go. I want this settled, and settled now."

"Now? After all these years you're in an all-fired hurry to settle it now?"

"Since I just learned I had a son less than ten minutes ago, yeah, Jolie. I'm in a big hurry to settle it now."

Jolie jammed her fists against her hips. Cord had to remember to breathe. Her cheeks were flushed and her green eyes sparked. The best sex they'd had was makeup sex after their fights. There'd been many. He'd forgotten that. The passage of time had smoothed over those memories so only the good ones stood out. But man, those particular bad times were so *good*!

Gesturing down the street toward the bank on the next

corner, Chance suggested adjourning to the conference room there. Cord had to stifle a laugh. His brother was being such a sneaky lawyer; the bank belonged to Barron Enterprises. Not exactly neutral territory. He could live with that. He needed every advantage, especially since he felt as if his world had tilted on its axis. At Jolie's nod, Chance pulled out his cell and made a call.

Cassie appeared with a foam box and winked at CJ. "So what's the plan?"

"We're going to the bank to use the conference room." Chance gripped the handles of Cord's wheelchair and started pushing.

Giggling, CJ squirmed so he was sitting facing forward. "Make it go fast?"

"No," all four adults answered simultaneously.

Once they were inside the bank, Cassie disappeared into the break room with CJ in tow. When Jolie followed, ready to argue, Cassie showed some of her own temper.

"Good grief. The kid is going to eat his strawberry short-cake in here. Do you seriously want him listening to the two of you slinging mud at each other? Really?"

There was a reason Cord loved his sister-in-law. She didn't take crap from anyone. Not his brothers, not Chance and definitely not his father. As he watched, some of the starch wilted out of Jolie, especially when Cass reached over to touch her arm.

"Look, Jolie, I get why you're nervous. I promise I'm just going to sit with him. We'll both be here when y'all get through talking. Okay?"

Jolie blinked several times, inhaled deeply and relaxed. "Okay."

And that was that. Jolie pivoted and marched toward the conference room door, where Chance and Cord were waiting. She brushed past them and a wisp of sweet mimosa scent followed in her wake. Cord had to shift in the chair to ease the fullness pressing against his zipper. He inhaled shallowly, but her scent still perfumed the air. He needed his head clear to deal with this situation.

On one level, he was so angry he wanted to punch something. But on another, the twisty, bendy parts of his psyche were plotting ways to use the fact they had a son together to his advantage. He wanted Jolie. He always had. Now he had leverage.

"I need some space." Cord stared at Chance.

"That's not a good idea."

"Get out, Chance. I want to talk to Jolie. Alone."

His brother wasn't very happy, as evidenced by the tense set of his shoulders and grim expression, but Chance did as he asked and vacated the conference room. Once they were alone and he was positive Chance didn't linger at the door to eavesdrop, Cord studied Jolie. She looked nervous. Defensive. And, oh, yeah, there was a healthy dose of guilt, too. That was good.

"What do you want, Cord?"

"I think it's pretty obvious."

"Well, it's not."

"I want to work things out. Between us. And I want something else, Jolie. Space."

Jolie watched Cord closely, waiting for the rest of his demands, but air escaped from her lungs in a soft whoosh of relief regardless. She could handle space between them. "Okay. Yeah. I guess that's a good thing."

When she'd first run into Cord at the restaurant, Jolie had never been so angry in her life. Despite moving back to Oklahoma City, despite harboring some romantic notion that Cord might have changed and that they might grab a second chance, she knew it to be the pipe dream of a naive girl. She no longer had stars in her eyes. She was a mother. And a darned good one. She'd brought CJ into this world all by herself and she'd taken care of him. All. By. Herself.

She didn't need Cord Barron. And she didn't want him to have a place in CJ's life.

Then she felt fear. Seeing her son sitting there in Cord's lap had panicked her. The Barrons were just as powerful as her father. Why had she been stupid enough to come home? It was inevitable that this would happen, and she'd been an idiot to believe otherwise.

But now it looked as if Cord was willing to give her some breathing room.

"I don't think you understand." Something hard glinted in Cord's eyes, a flash as bright and inevitable as lightning in a summer thunderstorm. "I want time, Jolie. Time with CJ. And the space to get to know him on my terms."

Was it possible to sweat icicles? To be so hot and cold at the same time? Jolie stared at him, the word *no* already forming on her lips.

"Do you really want to drag him through the court system?"

She sputtered and had to breathe through the surge of anger. "You'd do that to him?"

"To see my son? To spend time with him? To be acknowledged as his father? Damn straight I would. You've already cheated me out of so much, Jolie. You don't want to deny me this."

She forced her fingers to loosen from the fists they'd formed without her knowledge as she considered Cord's threat. The planes of his face looked as if they'd been carved from the alabaster stone that formed amid the red dirt of Western Oklahoma.

"I want to get to know my son. To make up for the parts of his life you stole from me."

Her eyes burned with a hot flush of tears, but she blinked them away. Straightening her shoulders, she pasted on her best poker face. "No."

Cord did nothing except raise one eyebrow as if to say, "Really, Jolie? You truly want to do this?" He wore the mask well but he looked so pale, so…wounded. He'd almost died from his injuries, but now she knew without a doubt that she'd ripped out his heart. Just as he'd ripped out hers.

Five

Cord didn't argue with Jolie. He rolled to the door, opened it and maneuvered his wheelchair out. Chance was leaning against the wall nearby but straightened immediately.

"What's the plan?"

Cord lifted his chin to indicate Jolie was right behind him and Chance offered an almost imperceptible nod. They'd talk later, and Cord would lay out his plan then. His brother knew him well and didn't press for an answer to his question.

Jolie huffed to a stop behind him, unable to squeeze around the chair without bumping into him. He stifled the smile threatening to reveal his thoughts. She'd thrown down the gauntlet, and he'd picked it up without hesitation.

Giggles drew his attention as his sister-in-law and CJ appeared at the end of the hall. The boy stomped toward them, stopping in front of Chance.

Rearing his head back, hands fisted on his hips, CJ stared up. "Who're you?"

"My name is Chance. I'm your—" He glanced at Cord before shifting his gaze to Jolie. "Your dad and I are brothers."

"What's that mean, Mommy?"

Jolie's eyes narrowed and her lips pursed. "I don't want to talk about this right now."

"But, Mommy—"

"He's your uncle, CJ. Okay?"

"Okay. Do I have more?"

"You do." Cord replied before Jolie could. "Besides Chance, there's Clay, Cash and Chase."

"Are they all grown-ups?"

"Yup."

CJ sighed and offered puppy-dog eyes. "Are there any other kids?"

Jolie choked, and Cord wondered if he'd have to perform the Heimlich maneuver, but then remembered he couldn't stand up to administer it. Instead, he grinned at the boy but watched Jolie's face. "Just you, CJ, but maybe your mom and I could work on that for you. Maybe a little sister." Oh, yeah, that got a rise out of her. He glanced back at his son.

His son—and wasn't that a kick in the pants—screwed up his face as if he'd just taken a swig of lemon juice. "No girls. Girls are yucky." CJ had the good graces to glance up at his mother and then over at Cassie. "Well…some girls are okay. Like Mommy and Miss Cassie."

Jolie's face turned red, and had they been in the cartoons, steam would be hissing from her ears. He'd forgotten how much fun it was to push her buttons.

Without pausing for breath or giving his mother a chance to respond, CJ launched into his next subject. "Miss Cassie has horses. Do you have horses…uh…?" At a loss for what to call him, CJ's voice trailed off.

"I do have horses, bubba. And you can ride them whenever you want." He reached for the boy and tugged him a little closer. "Not sure what to call me, right?" Big eyed, CJ nodded. "Well, *Dad* works. Or *Daddy*. Whatever you'd like."

"*Daddy.* I like that."

Jolie made a strangled noise and reached for CJ, but Cord ignored her. "I like that too, bubba."

"We have to go, CJ." Jolie was about to snap, judging by her tone of voice and expression.

"No. I wanna stay with Daddy."

Shoving the wheelchair out of her way, she took CJ's arm. "No. Not today." She glared at Cord, her expression promising retribution with a big dose of "not now, not ever."

Cord figured he had to be the most perverse man who ever lived, because fighting with Jolie had been something he missed. A lot. Forget the makeup sex that came after. There was something…exhilarating about seeing her color rise, her fists tighten and her stubborn chin jut toward him as her eyes flashed like broken glass under a hot summer sun.

"No. Not today," he agreed easily. "Tomorrow." He smiled at her but caught Chance rolling his eyes. His brother was extremely familiar with his expression and the tone of voice.

"Cord." She clenched CJ's hand.

"Jolie."

"We're leaving."

"I'm not stopping you, Jolie. But I will see CJ tomorrow. I'll send Chance to pick him up, bring him out to the ranch."

"No."

Cord shrugged as if her resistance meant nothing. It stung, but that didn't matter. Not in the long run. "You know what the alternative is."

"You're bluffing."

A rolling gasp of laughter escaped from his chest and exploded out of his mouth. "Then, you don't know me at all, Jolene. Have him ready by nine. If he's not, Chance's next stop will be the courthouse."

"Which it'll also be if the two of you aren't home, Jolene." Chance just had to butt in, but Cord had known he would and had counted on it.

He tuned out Jolie's blustering and smiled at CJ. "Wish I wasn't in this chair, bubba, but I'll still show you some of our horses, and if you want to ride, our foreman, Kaden, will help you." He tousled the boy's hair. "Okay?"

"Okay!" CJ launched into his arms and Cord had to blink

back the sting of tears. Barrons didn't cry, but damned if he didn't want to. He had a son. And he had the woman he loved, even though she didn't realize she was his. Yet.

Jolie seethed and just barely managed to contain her anger. She wanted to beat her fists against the steering wheel but CJ was strapped into his car seat behind her and could see her face in the rearview mirror.

How dare Cordell Barron swoop into her life and steal her son away? There was no way on God's green earth she would let the Barrons sink their claws into CJ. She needed to call her dad. He had a whole firm of high-priced lawyers at his beck and call. They could file an injunction or something. Make sure Cord wasn't allowed anywhere near her or CJ.

She suddenly went cold, as if a bucket of rainwater had been dumped over her head. Was her reaction about CJ? Or her? Not long ago, she'd fantasized about rekindling a relationship with Cord. Some fantasy! The reality of the man—the truth of what it would mean to share her son with him—hit her square in the heart. She couldn't do it. But the alternative meant hurting CJ. She'd have to figure out some way to deal with the situation without getting her heart—or her son's—broken.

She glanced in the rearview mirror and recognized the stubborn tilt of her son's chin. It was about the only thing he'd inherited from her. "How about we stop and buy a movie on the way home?"

"No."

Yes, her son's temperament hit a little too close to home. "But you want to see that new—"

"No. I'm mad at you, Mommy."

"Fine." Oh, great. Now she was getting snippy with a four-year-old.

"Fine," he snipped back.

When they got home, dinner and bath time were a bat-

tle. CJ refused to watch TV with her, holing up in his room
instead. When she went in to offer a bedtime story, he
crawled into bed, turned his back and ignored her.

Out of sorts, she sprawled on the overstuffed couch in
the area her Realtor called a media room. Some inane romantic comedy laugh tracked its way across the giant TV
screen affixed to the wall. The thing had come with the
house and there were times she enjoyed it. Tonight, not
so much. Pushing off the couch, Jolie paced around the
room, her thoughts as chaotic as the storm clouds gather-
ing outside. Deep down, she knew she didn't have a legal
leg to stand on. She couldn't prove Cord meant to harm CJ.
She couldn't ding him for lack of child support because he
hadn't known he was a father.

Her earlier conversation with her father as she was preparing dinner had been short, to the point and disappoint-
ing. And now she was mad at him because he seemed to
be taking Cord's side. Then again, he'd always gotten bib-
lical with her.

"You reap what you sow," he'd told her on numerous occasions, quickly followed up with his belief that she was
wrong for not telling Cord about CJ. Tonight, he'd told her
he'd hire an attorney to represent her in the paternity suit
they were both sure Cord would file.

Could she really do that to CJ? Drag him through the
newspapers, because they darn sure would glom onto the
story—the legitimate press *and* the tabloids. Possible headlines flashed across her thoughts and none of them were
pretty.

"Argh!" She wanted to hit something. Or throw something against the wall—something that would crash and
break into a million pieces. She had no choice. She needed
an attorney so the Barrons couldn't run roughshod over
her, but she would have to let Cord see her son. *Her* son.
Not his. She'd dealt with the three months of morning sickness. She'd brought CJ into the world with no help from

the Barrons. She'd dealt with his colic, teething, earaches and everything else. All by herself.

And whose fault is that? No matter what she did, she couldn't muffle the sound of her conscience.

"Okay!" She yelled the admission. "My fault. It's all my freaking fault! Are you happy now?"

No, she wasn't happy at all. But she had to face the consequences. She had to allow Cord to spend time with CJ. She blinked and a wry smile crinkled her cheeks. Cord was a Barron. Barrons never stuck with anything that even hinted at personal responsibility. They got bored too easily. And hated having to make an effort. They expected to snap their fingers and everybody would line up to do their bidding. Well, Cord had a lot to learn about being a father. Especially since his own father was such a lousy example.

Jolie did a short happy dance. That was the ticket. Cord would get bored with being a father, and once he had his fill, he'd ignore CJ. Her heart contracted, knowing CJ would more than likely get hurt. But better he discovered now what a jerk his father was than later, when he'd have a harder time getting over it. She shoved those uncomfortable feelings away. She never wanted to hurt CJ, but ever since Cordell Barron entered the picture, hurt was inevitable. For both of them.

She trudged to her room, doing her best to ignore her feelings about—and for—Cord. The man drove her to distraction. He always had. All he had to do was smile, and her knees went all wobbly while her heart raced and goose bumps prickled her skin. And when he touched her? Her pulse—and other places—throbbed with the thought. She needed a cold shower stat, and headed to the master bath.

Jolie had dated postbreakup with Cord, in an I'll-show-him way, and most often with disastrous results. Nursing school had convinced her she didn't have time for men. And then CJ. Men didn't want a woman with the baggage of another man's child. Not just *another man*. Cord. She balled her fists on the granite vanity top and stared at her reflection.

"Get over him, girl!"

Her brain could list all the reasons why she should tell him to take a flying leap, but her body was up in arms and rebelling. She *wanted* him in that hot, skin-to-skin seductive way a woman wants the man who inflames her inside and out. And darn if her heart wasn't standing there on the edge of the cliff ready to take the leap with her girlie bits.

She crawled into bed, hit the remote control and found a program guaranteed to bore her into sleep. Her dreams, however, were far from boring. Tangles of arms and legs, deep kisses until her lips were swollen and she couldn't catch her breath. Flushed, she pushed off the linen duvet coverlet and flopped onto her back, arms wide. The ceiling fan washed a desultory breeze over her that did nothing to dissipate the heat. The digital clock on her bedside table blinked an accusatory three-thirty in her direction.

The TV droned in the background, casting flickering shadows around the room. For a brief moment, Jolie wondered what Cord was doing. Focusing on the program, she thrust thoughts of the man out of her mind—at least until her brain processed what she was seeing on the screen. She'd gone to sleep to a documentary and awakened to a man and woman writhing in ecstatic, no-holds-barred, down-and-dirty sex on a dining room table.

"Really?" She didn't know whether to laugh, cry or get out the vibrator. She didn't believe in signs, but if ever there might be one, this would be her luck. Giving up on any chance of sleep, she shoved out of bed and padded into the bathroom.

Cord twisted his hips, first right then left. He followed up with some of the other exercises his physical therapist insisted he do. Sometimes his insides still felt like scrambled eggs, though at the moment, it was his thoughts that more closely resembled food. Spaghetti. A big ole knot of it, twisted and tangled.

"I have a son." He tested the words by saying them aloud. "I'm a father." That one didn't settle, as well. He wasn't a father. Thanks to Jolie. She'd made sure he missed out on those all-important early years with CJ. CJ. He wondered what the initials stood for. Surely she hadn't named the boy after him. He made a mental note to ask CJ when he saw him.

Tomorrow. Cord glanced at the clock. Today, he amended. He'd have the day to spend with his son. He glared at the insectile shadow looming against the far wall of his childhood bedroom. He hated that wheelchair with a passion bordering on rabid. He would be rid of it as soon as possible.

Despite the sweat beading on his forehead, he redoubled his efforts, lifting his legs, holding them elevated until his abdominal muscles screamed and he couldn't breathe. Lowering them to the bed, he panted until the pain passed.

As he rested, his thoughts turned to Jolie. A different kind of pain washed over him, one that was both physical and emotional. His body hardened as he remembered all too well the feel of her curves, the sound of her soft, panting breaths as they made love. There'd been girls before her and women after, but none of them ever stirred him like Jolie. Now that she was back, he seriously doubted there'd ever be another. But at the same time, she'd done the unthinkable. Had she gotten pregnant on purpose? He got mad just thinking about it.

His anger simmered just beneath the surface. He had every right to be furious with her, but he hadn't exactly been a knight in shining armor where she was concerned. He'd acquiesced to his father's demand that he break it off without a backward look. Well, maybe a few glances and a very heavy heart, but he'd been a coward. He could own up to the label now, especially in light of what his younger brother had done.

Up to his old tricks, Cyrus had declared Cassie Morgan's father an enemy, and when the man had died, Cyrus had turned all that venom on Cassie. The old man was determined to steal Cassie's inheritance right out from under her—and would have if not for Chance.

Cord curled his head up, bringing knees and elbows together in a modified sit up. Cyrus had underestimated Chance—and the depth of feelings he had for the pretty little cowgirl. Chance had stood up to their father and never even looked back. If Cord were honest, he'd admit his small part in the epic cattle drive and the ensuing drama at the stockyards had been liberating. Especially in light of his own gutless action when Cyrus had given him the ultimatum regarding Jolie.

As he worked through the rest of the exercises prescribed by the therapist, he daydreamed. What would his life be like if he'd told his old man to shove it? He pictured him and Jolie in a little house with a bunch of kids, him working in the oil patch. He'd be a great dad, playing with the kids, teaching them how to play football and baseball—even the girls. And the nights spent with Jolie in his arms? Oh, yeah. Now, there was a dream he could grab hold of.

Except.

Reality shoved its way into his reverie. Jolie wouldn't have been happy in a little house. And as a lowly roughneck, he wouldn't have been able to afford the lifestyle she was used to. She'd always wanted to go to nursing school. Her father would have helped, but Cord was self-aware enough to know he would have resented every penny J. Rand Davis gave them.

The sweat on his body chilled, and he grabbed a towel to wipe his face. His little brother was damned lucky. Cord shook his head. No, not lucky. Determined. And willing to stand up to their old man. Because of Cassie.

Chance and Cassie. They had a great thing going. His brother worshipped the ground his wife walked on. She'd tempered Chance. He smiled easier, laughed more often. Cord wanted that with a woman. He wanted that with Jolie. He always had. And he'd get it. One way or another. Because that was what Barrons did.

Six

Cord waited in the doorway of the barn, watching the shiny Mercedes SUV sweep up the drive. Behind him, CJ giggled as he helped the ranch manager, Kaden Waite, feed the horses. He figured it was Jolie in the vehicle, come to pick up their son. His heart contracted and then expanded at the thought. *Their son.* He'd known about CJ—whose full name was Cordell Joseph, though according to CJ, he was only called that when he was in trouble—for less than a day, but already the kid owned him heart and soul. He'd do anything for this child. Hell, he'd do anything for Jolie. All he had to do was convince her they belonged together. The three of them. One happy family.

He lost sight of the SUV as it parked in the circle drive in front of the sprawling stacked-stone-and-log ranch house. Moments later, his cell phone dinged with a text from Miz Beth, the Barron family's longtime cook and substitute mother figure.

U HAV CMPANY

The woman hated to text, but she didn't like calling one of the boys in front of people, either.

Cord texted back, asking if it was Jolie.

u nED to ComE NOW

Miz Beth's message was plain, despite her typos. "CJ, we need to head to the house."

"But I'm not finished helpin' Mr. Kaden, Daddy."

Cord's breath caught in his chest when he heard that word on CJ's lips. "He can finish up, bubba. Someone's up at the big house waitin' for us."

"Who?" CJ dragged his feet but approached.

"Not sure, but Miz Beth says we need to get up there pronto."

Kaden had followed CJ out of the barn. "I'll bring the UTV around, Cord."

The other man ducked back inside and returned moments later driving a two-seat utility vehicle with a bed on the back big enough to hold the wheelchair. After a bit of maneuvering, and more help from Kaden than he wanted to admit he needed, Cord, CJ and the chair were bouncing along the gravel road back to the main house. He stopped at the back, where Miz Beth's husband, Big John, met them.

A few minutes later, he rolled through the house while CJ darted ahead.

"Grandy!"

Grandy? Who was here? Expecting Jolie, Cord worked to school his expression as he turned the corner to find J. Rand Davis standing in the entry hall. Miz Beth stood her ground, chin jutted, hands on hips, blocking Rand from coming any farther into the house. The older man's eyes flicked in Cord's direction.

"Cordell."

"Mr. Davis."

"Grandy, Grandy. Guess what I did!" CJ all but leaped into his grandfather's arms, demanding his attention.

Without taking his eyes off Cord, Rand said, "No clue, CJ. What did you do?"

"I fed horses! And got to sit on one while Mr. Kaden led him around the corral."

Rand ruffled the boy's hair affectionately. "Sounds like you had a fine time today, CJ. Ready to go home?"

"Aww, do I hav'ta, Grandy?"

Cord realized Rand was waiting for him to say something. He cleared his throat. "Since your grandfather drove all the way out here to get you, bubba, yeah, time to go home." Before CJ could launch into an argument, he continued, "But tell ya what. I'll call your mom and see about maybe you coming out and spending the weekend, okay?"

"Like a sleepover?"

"Yeah, like a sleepover."

"Cool."

Rand glanced at the housekeeper, noted her apron with a tilt of his head and sniffed the air, which was filled with scents of apple and cinnamon. "Are those apple fritters I smell?"

"They surely are." The woman, always astute, glanced between Cord and Rand before holding out her hand. "CJ, honey, why don't you come with me to the kitchen. I have some fritters and milk for you to eat before you head home."

The boy squirmed loose from his grandfather and happily joined her. Once they were out of sight and hearing, Rand said, "We need to talk, Cordell."

Jolie paced her kitchen. At one end of her path, she checked the time on the chrome-and-neon clock on the wall. After pivoting and marching back to the far side of the room, she checked her watch. When the phone rang, she all but jumped out of her skin. She snagged the receiver and answered with a worried "Hello?"

"Jolie, it's Cord."

As if she wouldn't recognize his voice. Pleasure warred with panic. "Is CJ okay?"

"He's fine. Your father picked him up about twenty minutes ago. He mentioned something about hamburgers before bringing him home."

"I swear my dad spoils that boy rotten."

Cord chuckled, and the sound melted her bones. "It's easy to do. He's an awesome kid." Silence stretched as she tried to figure out what to say. Luckily, Cord beat her to it. "Ah…thanks."

His gratitude perplexed her. "For what?"

"For letting CJ come to the ranch. For giving me a chance."

She bit back the retort on the tip of her tongue. Something about his voice tugged at her heart. He sounded uncertain. "You're welcome, Cord."

"Can we talk, Jolie?"

Yes, it *was* uncertainty she caught in his voice, and the idea that Cordell Barron might be uncertain about anything rocked her back on her heels. She expected him to be demanding. Arrogant. Confident. All the things he'd always been around her. But uncertain? He'd been so sure of himself in high school. College. Even the night of their hookup. He'd been positive she'd stay the night, that they'd fall back into their relationship. She steeled her emotions even as her skin tingled in remembrance of that night.

"What do you want to talk about, Cord?"

"Our son."

No hesitation on his part. *Our* son. Those words seared her soul like the hot Oklahoma wind.

"I really want to be CJ's dad. I want to spend time with him. Do things and get to know him. Make up for lost time, you know?"

Now he was tugging on her guilty conscience, so she said nothing but a noncommittal "Mmm."

"Can we do this without getting the lawyers involved?"

Still she didn't answer, marshaling her chaotic thoughts. She didn't want to share CJ. She didn't. Especially not with the Barrons. The Barrons… Okay, *Cyrus* Barron was the problem. That horrid old man was nothing but poison when it came to his own sons. She sighed inwardly because Cord was right. CJ was his son, too.

"We have a son together, Jolie. Can't we be friends, at least?"

"I don't know, Cord. I'm not sure that's a good idea." Jolie wanted to bite her tongue. Why did she continue to antagonize him? Cord sincerely wanted to get to know CJ. Even so, she was reluctant to trust him. In addition to the fact he once broke her heart, and could do so again if she wasn't careful, she couldn't get past his last name and the fact that Cyrus would have access to CJ. Yet Cord appeared, at the moment, to be acting reasonable about things. Mostly. Okay, definitely. She was the one being a witchy woman, her broken heart notwithstanding. She had every reason to be cautious. Right? Right.

"You're thinking too hard, sunshine."

Sunshine. Her tummy did a cartwheel and she sank down on the nearest bar stool. "You haven't called me that in…forever."

"I haven't talked to you in forever. Not really. You never stuck around my hospital room long enough."

He'd reached out to her as he'd lain racked with pain in that bed, and while part of her turned all warm and fuzzy with the memory, the hurt and heartbroken girl she'd buried all those years ago wouldn't let go of her anger.

"You're still thinking too hard." Cord's voice was thick and husky with emotion, and for the first time, she wondered if their breakup had hurt him, too. That was a place she wasn't ready to explore.

"I know. I have a lot to think about."

An uncomfortable silence reared its head again, and the tension made Jolie fidget. She had so many questions she wanted to ask, but wasn't sure she wanted the answers.

"I should let you go. Tell CJ I love him and sweet dreams when you put him to bed tonight. And…tell him I'll ask you another time about spending the weekend with me." Breath hissed softly from between her lips and Cord inhaled. The moment was as intimate as a kiss. "G'night, sunshine."

The broken connection hummed in her ear before she could respond. Jolie dashed at her eyes, irritated that tears threatened to spill over and drown her cheeks. If she ever succumbed to tears, she'd never stop.

Cord put down the phone and pushed himself up on the bed. God, but she still turned him on. Just her voice had the ability to twist him into a hot mess of nerves and made him want things he'd walked away from, and probably couldn't have again. Like her. In his bed. In his life. But the yearning just made him more resolute. He would make them a family.

He swung his legs over and steadied himself on the edge of the mattress. Today with CJ had been a breath of fresh air, but he'd overdone things physically. Eyeing the wheelchair with something akin to hatred, he braced one hand on the sturdy wooden footboard of his bed and eased into a standing position.

So far, so good. He had fifteen steps to the bathroom. Three of those were close to the footboard. After that, he was on his own in uncharted territory. He hadn't taken a step since the accident without a physical therapist and safety equipment holding him. He hadn't even tried a walker yet, but talking to Jolie, listening to her breathe into the phone did more than just make him aware of how sexy she was. It made him want to get well, to be the man who had once took her to bed and left her panting and moaning his name against his shoulder.

His talk with Rand Davis had also left him off balance— and wondering what Jolie's father was up to. Not to mention leaving Cord questioning everything that had happened between him and Jolie for the past ten years.

Leaning heavily on the footboard, he shuffled toward his bathroom. He paused and stared at the door across the open floor. So near yet so far. But he was sick and tired of being an invalid. If he was going to be a real dad to CJ, if he had any chance of winning Jolie back, he had to suck it up.

Agonizing minutes later, sweating like a racehorse after the Kentucky Derby, he leaned on the cool granite counter and stared at his reflection in the mirror. He'd lost weight and muscle tone, and the gray pallor did not blend well with his fading tan. Time to rectify things. From now on, he was standing on his own two feet. Well, with the help of a walker, but not for long. Nope, not for long at all.

An hour later, he entered the kitchen, standing on his own two feet, though pushing the wheeled walker the therapist had sent over. Miz Beth sniffled and waved him to the broad breakfast bar while she hustled up a plate and silverware. Big John moved the walker back out of the way as Cord settled into one of the tall chairs fronting the bar. A few minutes later, Kaden sauntered in and washed up at the kitchen sink.

The three men shuffled food into their mouths with no time for polite conversation between bites. But after dinner, when Miz Beth served warm apple fritters and coffee, Cord broached a new subject with the ranch manager.

"What do you know about therapeutic riding, Kaden?"

The other man shrugged. "Read some stuff. Saw it when I was up at Oklahoma State gettin' my degree." Kaden turned to face him, a thoughtful expression knitting his brow and pursing his lips. "You thinkin' about getting back in the saddle, boss man?"

Cord barely refrained from rolling his eyes. He and his brothers had known almost from the moment Kaden had been hired that he was a Barron, despite his last name being the same as his mother's—Waite. The Chickasaw half of his heritage explained his tanned skin and black hair, but his eyes—like all the offspring of Cyrus Barron—gave him away. To Cord's knowledge, Kaden never mentioned his father, and definitely never acknowledged he might be

Cyrus Barron's son. Raised by a mother who'd never married, Kaden kept his own counsel and ran the ranch's cattle and horse operations like a man with twice his experience.

"Yeah, I am. Maybe teach CJ to ride at the same time."

Cord caught Kaden's flickering glance before the man answered, "We can do that." Kaden took a long drag on the coffee in his cup and swallowed before facing Cord. "You sure seem to be acceptin' of this situation, Cord."

"He's my son, Kaden. I'm not going to turn my back on him." *Or his mother.*

Taking another swallow, Kaden stood up. "Mighty fine dinner, Miz Beth. Thank you." He tipped an invisible hat to Big John before clapping a gentle hand on Cord's shoulder. "That's what makes you different, Cordell Barron. It surely does."

Seven

More nervous than a sinner sitting in the front pew, Cord waited on the porch of the main house. Jolie had agreed to let CJ stay the weekend at the ranch. He'd had almost two weeks to get used to having a son. While he was excited to see CJ, it was the anticipation of seeing Jolie and putting his plan into action that had his nerves twanging. Dinner first, with Jolie staying to eat, and then maybe the three of them watching a movie. To ease any nerves the boy might have about sleeping in a new place. That was Cord's excuse. It all sounded plausible to him. Surely Jolie was nervous, too, about leaving her son with virtual strangers.

John and Miz Beth had set up the patio for grilling burgers, all within easy walking distance so Cord wouldn't have to rely on the walker. He'd already mostly abandoned it, but for longer distances. In addition to burgers and hot dogs ready to be slapped on the grill, there was Miz Beth's famous potato salad. Sweet tea—Jolie's favorite—and fruit punch. A tub of homemade ice cream in the freezer. All that was lacking in his perfect scenario was Jolie and CJ.

He'd loved Jolie with an unreasonable fervor when they were younger. And he'd been a dreamer. The old man had put a stop to that. Cord shook off that train of thought. He couldn't go back and change the past. All he could do was work toward the future he wanted. Thoughts of his father filled his chest with cold dread. Thankfully, he was down in Houston looking at an oil refinery to buy. Cord should be there with him, as CEO of BarEx, and would have been but for his accident.

But it was good his father was away. So far, it seemed as if no one had spilled the beans about CJ. That wouldn't last, and when Cyrus found out, hell would certainly break loose. With luck, Cord's plan would work and he'd have Jolie and CJ back before the old man could do a thing to stop him.

The cool night wind prickled the hair on his arms. It was just the wind—or so he told himself. Not a premonition about his father.

Cord went back to his strategy for tonight. Maybe he'd opt for s'mores around the patio's fire pit instead of a movie. His chest tightened, along with his groin, at the thought of snuggling with Jolie on the big lounger. Every night, he slipped into sleep with her eyes and beautiful body foremost in his thoughts. He dreamed of touching her skin and always woke up hard and hungry. And not just since his accident.

Tires crunching on gravel pulled him out of his reverie. He ducked back into the shadows to watch the woman he still loved and their son arrive. As Jolie's crossover SUV swung into the big circle, he ducked through the front door. Wouldn't do to let her see his anxiety. He almost laughed out loud. Anxious? Hell, he was terrified he'd screw this up. And if he did? There'd be no second chance.

When the car rolled to a smooth stop before the wide front steps, he opened the door and strode forward, a mask of confidence plastered on his face. He'd worked his ass off for two weeks to lose the chair and the walker. He couldn't go far, but by damn he could get to the porch and down the steps. Luckily, he hadn't taken the first riser when CJ barreled into him.

"Dad! Dad! Mom! Mom! Lookie. See!" The boy whirled toward his mom, his face alight with happiness. "Daddy's walkin'!"

"I can see that." Jolie quirked an eyebrow as if she didn't believe her eyes. "Don't you think it's a little soon?"

"Nope. The therapist told me to go at my own speed."

"Daddy, Daddy, Dad." CJ tugged at his pants' leg to get his attention. "Can we play ball now? Mom won't play."

That was Cord's cue to quirk his brow. "Really? Huh." He knew damn well Jolie had been an all-state softball player who threw harder than many of the guys in their high school.

Jolie rolled her eyes as she popped the rear hatch and dragged out a backpack, a little wheeled suitcase and a very large floppy dog. She carried everything to the top of the steps and handed the stuffed animal to CJ and the backpack to Cord. "I haven't had time."

"Do you have time now?"

Jolie narrowed her gaze. "To play ball?"

"No, to stay for dinner."

She opened her mouth to decline but CJ jumped in to rescue him. "Please, Mommy?" He bobbed his head in an emphatic nod. "What're we havin'? Is Miss Beth cookin'?"

"Nope, bubba. Me. I have the grill fired up for some burgers and hot dogs." He adopted CJ's winsome expression and turned it on Jolie. "Please? Miz Beth did make homemade ice cream, and if it gets any cooler, I thought maybe we could roast marshmallows and make s'mores. You used to love s'mores." He was not above wheedling shamelessly.

"Please, Mommy. You fix my stuff just right. You can show Daddy. Right, Daddy?" CJ transferred his tugs from Cord's jeans to his hand.

"Right, CJ."

"Don't you think for a minute I don't know what you're up to, Cordell Barron."

CJ giggled, and both adults looked at him. "Are you in trouble?"

Laughing, Cord hefted the backpack up on his shoulder

so he could ruffle the boy's hair without letting go of his hand. "I'm pretty much always in trouble with your mom, bubba." He glanced at Jolie but she wouldn't meet his gaze. "So how 'bout it, Mom? Will you stay for dinner?"

"I have to go."

"So you have plans?" Cord worked to keep his poker face in place. "Stay for dinner, Jolie. Help CJ get settled in, 'kay?"

She narrowed her eyes, and he fully expected her to start shaking her "mother finger" at him. Miz Beth always did when she knew he'd been up to something nefarious.

"Please, Mommy? Pretty please with gummy worms and whipped cream on top?"

Laughing, Jolie put one hand on her hip in mock dismay. "You're the one who likes gummy worms, CJ."

"Yeah, your mom's weakness is white chocolate."

A flicker of surprise crossed her expression and Cord wondered why. He remembered everything about her.

"Nothing's going to happen, Cord." Yet he saw the moment she capitulated.

He did his best to look innocent before turning toward the front entrance. CJ trotted along, still holding his hand. When the two of them reached the massive wooden door, they both turned to check on Jolie. She still stood rooted to the spot where they'd left her.

"S'mores, Mom." CJ had his best look of entreaty firmly in place.

Cord grinned and winked. "Yeah, Mom. S'mores. I even have white chocolate for yours."

Jolie threw up her hands, grabbed the handle of the suitcase and dragged it along with her. She laughed when Cord and CJ high-fived and did her best to nip the warm feelings budding inside her. She'd wanted this her whole life—this teasing closeness that families had. Well, families other than her own. An only child, she'd envied her friends their siblings, including Cord with all his brothers

and cousins. One big rowdy family. Like musketeers. She'd
wanted to be a musketeer.

Leaving CJ's paraphernalia tucked into an alcove in the
entry hall, Cord ushered them through the house toward
the back patio. Jolie dragged her feet, turning in the oc-
casional circle to see everything. She'd never been inside.
There were soaring ceilings with open beams, a stacked
stone fireplace, oversize leather couches and chairs, thick
rugs on the heart of pine floor. Native American and Western art adorned the walls.

They passed a formal dining room with a deer-antler
chandelier and she got a peek at the gourmet kitchen before Cord opened the French doors leading to the flagstone
patio. There was an outdoor kitchen nicer than most people
had in their homes out there.

Cord played the perfect host. He'd thought of everything. Drinks—red fruit punch for CJ, sweet tea with a
fresh slice of orange for her. A tray with fixings for their
burgers. Chili and cheese.

And then there was the man himself, presiding over
the grill while CJ played with one of the ranch dogs and
she lounged near the fire pit crackling with piñon wood.
How many times had she dreamed of just such a scenario
back when she was young and dumb? More times than she
wanted to admit.

A beautiful heated pool was built into the edge of the
patio. Steam rose as the temperature continued to cool, and
the lulling sound of a man-made waterfall murmured in
the background. Beyond the pool, a beautifully landscaped
yard stretched toward the working part of the ranch—
barns, corrals and cottages where the ranch hands lived. It
was a revelation, and she understood now why all the Barron brothers loved the place. The mansion in Nichols Hills
had been their residence during the school year. The ranch
was their home. Christmas. Birthdays. Summer vacations.

Jolie had attended parties at the Nichols Hills house.

She'd never been invited to the ranch. Until now. She didn't want to wonder why, didn't want the insecurity, anger and hurt from that long-ago time to rear its ugly head. Tonight they could be friends. They could share her son… She sighed and rethought that. Their son. Being honest, she was terrified Cord would somehow steal CJ away, turn him against her the way Cyrus Barron had turned Cord. And she wasn't ready to share CJ's affection, even as she watched him run to Cord and throw his arms around his dad's thighs and babble excitedly.

She didn't want to see the honest emotion on Cord's face as he listened patiently, as his hand rested on CJ's head, fingers mussing hair the exact same color as his. She didn't have to see their eyes to know they were two peas in a pod. Barron DNA didn't fall far from the tree.

"Mom!"

She blinked from her reverie to realize that CJ had called her several times and now stood in front of her, hands on his hips. "What, baby?"

"I'm not a baby. Daddy says food's ready. I need you to fix my hot dog, 'cept I wanna try some chili and some cheese and lots and lots of mustard."

Jolie glanced at Cord. Chili was his condiment of choice. He ate it on his hamburgers. Hot dogs. Eggs. He'd probably put it on ice cream if the ice cream wouldn't melt. She pushed off the lounger and walked over to the counter next to the built-in grill. With CJ telling her exactly how much of everything he wanted, she fixed his plate and installed him at the wrought iron table, cloth napkin firmly tied around his neck. When she returned to start putting together her own meal, Cord handed a plate to her. Hamburger with sliced Parmesan cheese, Romaine lettuce and Caesar dressing.

He remembered. How did he do that? And did he realize she hadn't eaten a burger dressed this way since they'd broken up? Her throat closed and burned as she blinked back unwanted tears. This was the man she remembered—the sweet one who spoiled her. But she really needed to remember the bastard who'd ripped out her heart and then stomped on it, grinding it beneath the heels of his expensive Western boots.

"Mom!" CJ stood up in his chair, waving his arms at her. "C'mon, Mom. I'm hungry."

"Go sit down, sunshine. I'll refill your tea and be right there."

With a warm hand on the small of her back, Cord urged her toward the table. Did he know? Could he feel the blood rushing through her veins so fast it pounded in her ears? She hoped not. She needed every advantage to keep him at arm's length.

Dinner was a blur, so much so she didn't even fuss at CJ for blowing bubbles—egged on by Cord—through the straw in his fruit punch. He ate everything on his plate and asked for seconds. This time his father fixed his hot dog. Perfectly, just as he'd done with her burger. Ice cream followed, and then CJ headed out into the yard dotted with lights to play tag and fetch with the dog, a huge, shaggy beast of indiscriminate heritage.

"You realize he's going to want a dog now, right?"

"What?" She glanced over as Cord settled onto the giant lounger next to her. His burned-honey eyes glowed warm and tempting in the incandescent shine from the landscape lights.

"He's going to bug you for a dog."

She chuckled. "And? He's been doing that practically from the time he could talk. Why do you think I had to drag Ducky out here?"

Cord got that sexy amused expression that used to melt her panties. "Ah, would that be the shapeless lump of fake fur napping in the entry?"

"Yup."

"Ducky?"

"He's a big *Marmaduke* fan but couldn't pronounce the name. He finally shortened it to Ducky."

"A kid after my own heart."

Jolie rolled her eyes. "Don't tell me you still watch cartoons…"

Cord laughed and every muscle in her body wanted to sing with joy as the sound washed over her. "I could be perfectly happy with only one channel on TV, so long as it was the Cartoon Network."

She let out a snorting giggle—but then wondered what he wore to watch toons in. Did he still wear those fitted cotton boxers—the ones that cupped his butt and hugged his thighs the way she wanted to do? She licked her bottom lip before catching it between her teeth. When she glanced up, she almost recoiled from the look of stark hunger on Cord's face.

Pulling back, Cord rolled to an unsteady stand. After a moment, he regained his balance and turned to tend the fire before calling to CJ.

"Hey, bubba, 'bout time for s'mores, yeah?"

The boy whooped and ran toward them. When he slid to a stop, Cord steadied him away from the fire pit. "Why don't you come inside with me? You can wash your hands and then you can help me bring out the stuff."

"Okeydoke."

Left alone, Jolie inhaled deeply. Several times. She smoothed her hair back from her face with shaking hands. That had been way too close for comfort. She'd wanted to throw herself into Cord's arms, kiss him, be kissed by him. All the feelings she'd suppressed for so many years bubbled up and were within a hairbreadth of boiling out. That wouldn't do. Wouldn't do at all.

By the time Cord and CJ returned, she'd reined in her emotions, stilled her trembling hands and smoothed her expression to hide the turmoil—as much from herself as from Cord. She could not—*would* not—walk down this path again. Her heart wouldn't survive if he turned on her again. Their history taught her to be a realist, and reality dictated Cord would do exactly what Cyrus Barron demanded. Always.

Eight

Cord left CJ arguing with Miz Beth and Big John about whether Dusty, the ranch dog, could come into the house to sleep on the boy's bed. He refused to make a bet on who'd win that one. Instead, he walked Jolie out to her car, albeit with a great deal of reluctance. Her arm brushed against his and heat flashed through him. He heard her breath hitch and wondered if their casual contact had the same effect on her. He hoped so.

He held her elbow as they descended from the porch, and while he wanted to drag his feet, it was Jolie who slowed as they walked around her car to the driver's door. He reached around her to open it but didn't get the chance when she leaned up against the vehicle. Chuckling, he stepped back from her so as not to crowd.

"Something funny?"

He offered a crooked grin and was gratified when her eyes lit up and focused on his mouth. "Does this feel as awkward to you as it does to me?"

"Awkward?"

"Yeah. Like first-date awkward. You know. Should I kiss her? Do I have bad breath? What happens if we both tilt our heads the same way and we bump noses, or…" He paused to sigh dramatically. "What if we bump teeth?"

Jolie's laugh was rich and deep and sincere—exactly the effect he was hoping for. "Do guys really worry about all that?"

Cord nodded solemnly. "Absolutely. And let's not even talk about boners."

That elicited a peal of laughter. "Seriously?"

"Oh, hell, yeah. Talk about awkward! When you're sixteen, an erection is pretty much a given whenever you're around a pretty girl. Trying to kiss and hide your arousal takes far more coordination than most teenage boys can manage."

Her eyes danced with devilish lights. "What about grown-up men?"

"Wait. Isn't that an oxymoron?"

She lightly slapped his arm before her fingers trailed across his chest only to finally drop back to her side. "Are you telling me men never grow up?"

"Yup. 'Fraid so. When it comes to pretty women, men are perpetual sixteen-year-olds."

"Horrors."

Cord realized his fingers had curled into his palms in an effort to keep from touching Jolie. This teasing banter was familiar, natural, the way they used to be. As he watched, he saw her shiver. The wind carried a real chill now, and her short sleeves did little to keep her protected from its cold fingers. Without thinking, he reached for her and ran his hands up and down her goose-bumped arms to create some friction heat.

Jolie leaned into him, and he forced his feet to remain planted on the driveway. Every sinew in his body strained to step closer, to press against the length of her body and hold her close. Just when he thought he'd lose the battle, she did the unthinkable. She stepped to him, her arms circling his waist. He gathered her close and buried his nose in her soft hair, inhaling the scent of mimosa and warm spring days. His heart thudded, and he could feel hers softly echo even through the flannel shirt he wore. Cord was afraid to speak, afraid of breaking the tentative connection humming between them. He felt her smile against his chest.

"Awkward," she mumbled, and chuckled, even as she pressed closer to his arousal.

He laughed. "Aah…perpetually sixteen. What can I say?" He sobered a moment later and whispered into her hair, "Thank you."

"For what?"

"For tonight. For dinner. For letting CJ stay the weekend." There was so much more he wanted to tell her, to thank her for. Mainly for carrying his child—when it would have been so easy not to—for raising him to be the funny, bright, amazing kid who was at that very moment convincing Miz Beth to let a shaggy, flea-infested ranch mongrel not only into her spotless house, but into bed with him. But Cord couldn't put all those feelings into words. Not yet.

When Jolie leaned back and raised her face, she stared at him for a long time, her eyes searching his expression. The moment she closed her eyes, he knew. She was waiting for his kiss. Brushing his lips across hers, he tightened his arms, and then let her go. Her eyelids popped open and she regarded him with puzzlement. Cord smoothed his thumb along the ridge of her cheekbone before catching a stray strand of hair and tucking it behind her ear.

I missed you. I want you. I need you. The words tumbled in his mind. He searched for his anger, his sense of betrayal, but her nearness overwhelmed those emotions. He never did have any sense of preservation where Jolie was concerned. If he truly was the son his old man wanted, he'd be plotting revenge simply because that was what Barrons did. But he couldn't—not the way Cyrus would. He wanted Jolie. He wanted his son. And he'd have them even if he had to play a little dirty to get them.

He wouldn't voice those hidden feelings out loud. Jolie would run for the hills if he did. It was too soon. He knew that, and if his plan had any hope of working, he had to keep those thoughts to himself.

"What?" The word feathered across his skin as Jolie exhaled.

"Hmm?" He was suddenly lost in her gaze.

"What are you thinking?"

He blinked and straightened, focusing on the here and now. A laugh escaped before he could swallow it. "Yeah, no. I'm not going there."

"What are you afraid of?"

Cord hid the cringe twisting his muscles. This conversation reminded him far too much of the games he played with his brothers. It always started with that question and quickly devolved into "I dare you" followed by "I double dare you." Those challenges never ended well. One or more brothers ended up at the ER and the rest whipped and grounded for life.

What *was* he afraid of? Simple answer—never seeing Jolie and CJ again. Of being stupid and messing things up—again—so that she left. Of spending the rest of his life without her, alone.

"More than you realize, sunshine." He pulled her closer and rested his forehead against hers. "More than you could know."

Her arms slipped back around his waist and she hooked her thumbs in his belt loops. "I wish you'd talk to me."

"I wish I could."

His honesty startled her into growing still, though her curiosity wouldn't let things stay that way. "You know, Cord, it's pretty easy. You just open your mouth and words come out."

"Easy for you to say." His wry chuckle disguised the tremor threatening his voice.

Jolie sighed and dropped her hands in preparation of pulling away from him. He tightened the arm around her waist and kissed her forehead before stepping back. "I would like to talk, Jolie. We sort of got off on the wrong foot."

The huff of angry air she blew out was just as expressive as her frustrated sigh moments ago. "Look, I know you want me to apologize—"

He held up his hands, cutting her off. "No. It's too late for that." Even in the dark, under the reddish glow of mercury vapor security lights, he could see her color rise. He backed up and half turned away as he tunneled fingers through his unruly hair. "Don't, Jolie."

Cord actually heard her jaw snap shut. Jamming his hands into his hip pockets, he stared up at the moon. Out here, away from city lights, the Oklahoma sky was a swathe of black satin dotted with diamonds while the giant pearl of a moon hung from a chain of clouds. Resisting the urge to sigh as loudly as she had, he watched her from the corner of his eye.

"This isn't easy for either of us. Yes, I'm still mad. And hurt. But you got hurt, too." He held up a hand to stay her arguments. "Just listen, okay? You're the one who wanted me to talk."

Closing her mouth, Jolie crossed her arms, lifting and plumping her breasts. When his gaze zeroed in on her chest, she growled at him and he laughed.

"Permanently sixteen, remember? If you stand there emphasizing them, I'm gonna look, babe. I'm a man. We like looking at pretty women. That's how we roll." He sobered and offered a conciliatory smile. "What's done is done, Jolie. All we can do now is move forward, right?"

She nodded with one quick downward jerk of her stubborn chin. It wasn't much to work with, but better than nothing, so he continued, "Now that I know about CJ, I want to be in his life. I want to be his father." He ruffled one hand through his hair again. "I had a piss-poor example, so I damn sure want to do a better job. We need to talk—maybe not tonight, but soon. About…things. About custody and support and stuff."

Cord didn't like the way her back stiffened when she asked, "Stuff?"

"Yeah, Jolie. Stuff. I want us to be friends. Or at least friendly." Oh, he wanted a whole helluva lot more than that, but he wasn't ready to play all his cards yet. "CJ needs two parents. And he deserves two parents who aren't at each other's throats all the time." He breathed a little easier when she visibly relaxed and appeared to consider what he said.

"CJ and I have gotten along just fine without you." She sounded defensive.

He swallowed the angry retort forming on the tip of his tongue. Instead, he watched her, the silent weight of his thoughts leaking into his gaze until she looked away, no longer defiant. She dropped her arms and fumbled behind her for the door handle.

"Why did you come back?"

Jolie froze. "What do you mean?"

"Just what I asked. What made you leave Houston, come back here?"

She scuffed her toe against the cobblestone driveway and refused to look at him. She mumbled something he couldn't quite make out so he nudged her again. "Jolie? Why?"

"I was homesick, okay?" She shifted from foot to foot and looked distinctly uncomfortable.

Cord grabbed her hand and tugged gently. "If we're going to talk tonight, we might as well be comfortable. Come back inside. You can kiss CJ good-night and we'll go out on the patio, talk out there in private."

"I need to go."

"Are you working tomorrow?"

"No."

"Have a hot date?"

"No!"

"Then what are *you* afraid of?" Oh, he'd very neatly turned the tables on her. Jolie flattened her lips into a grimace. "Certainly not you. Fine. Of course, if CJ complains and wants to come home with me, you have no one to blame but yourself."

He walked her back up the front steps, his palm a warm brand on the small of her back. Jolie prayed he didn't feel the shiver dancing through her. How was it possible he could still make her knees wobble? Even when she was furious with him, her heart thudded not from the fury but from lust. She craved him, no ifs, ands or buts.

Holding the front door, he let her precede him into the entry hall before leading the way up the stairs to the private part of the house—the bedrooms. Some of the doors were open—though there were no lights on inside—and she did her best not to gawk. She couldn't help but wonder which room Cord currently occupied. That way led to disaster. Her nights were already fraught with memories—the two of them in bed, on a blanket at the lake, in his apartment in college, in hotel rooms.

She was so engrossed in her thoughts, she ran into Cord's broad back when he stopped. She stumbled and he quickly whirled to grab and steady her.

"Shh." He held his finger to his lips. Cord nodded toward the open door of a bedroom.

Jolie peeked inside. A night-light cast a soft glow over the room. CJ, snuggly in his flannel pajamas, was sound asleep. One arm was thrown over the back of the shaggy mutt occupying the bed next to her son. She had to clap a hand over her mouth to stifle a giggle. Tiptoeing over, she swept her hair back so she could bend to place a kiss on CJ's cheek. Before she could, the dog licked her arm and she couldn't catch the laugh.

"Mommy?" CJ's eyes fluttered, and she smoothed the hair off his forehead.

"G'night, sweetheart. Mommy loves you," she said, kissing him.

"Night, Mommy. G'night, Daddy."

"G'night, bubba. Sweet dreams."

Cord stood beside her, ruffling the dog's fur with one hand and cupping the back of CJ's head with the other. She sucked in a breath as her heart seemed to freeze. How many times had she dreamed of this moment—of the two of them standing beside CJ's bed wishing him good-night? The dreams didn't even come close to the reality. Emotion swamped her and she turned away before Cord saw the tears glittering in her eyes. She stumbled out to the hallway and leaned against the wall, breathing heavily and dashing the back of her hand against her cheeks.

"Jolie? Honey, what's wrong?"

Before she knew what was happening, Cord pulled her into his arms and her cheek found its favorite resting spot against his shoulder. "Nothing," she murmured.

"Mmm-kay."

He obviously didn't believe her but didn't press for an answer. Instead, he tucked her under his arm and moved her down the stairs and into the great room. He guided her outside to the patio and settled her on the double lounger before disappearing back inside the house. Cord returned a few minutes later with a glass mug topped with whipped cream. Irish coffee. Damn the man. His memory was far too perfect. She accepted his offering and cupped it in her hands while he poked flames back to life in the fire pit.

Cord joined her on the lounger without asking. She didn't argue. Part of her needed his nearness much more than the part wanting him far, far away. He held a longneck beer bottle and offered her a toast.

"To what?"

"To...our son."

How could she resist that? She clinked her mug against the bottle, then took a sip. Her Irish coffee was as perfect as if she'd made it herself. Jolie didn't want to bring up the past, but the present was still too nerve-racking and the future was something she refused to contemplate. Being a coward, she lay against the nest of pillows at her back, watching flames dance along the fragrant piñon wood in the fire pit and sipping her drink.

Despite her best efforts to stop it, a tear perched on the ends of her lashes. This was what she'd dreamed of—evenings like this with Cord, the two of them sharing comfortable silences while their little one slept just inside. She'd wanted what all her friends wanted. A man who loved her, whom she loved. A man who wanted to spend a lifetime making her happy. But she'd fallen in love with Cordell Barron, the one man she could never have.

Cord relieved her of the cup and slipped his arm beneath her shoulders, snuggling her closer to his side. "Don't cry, baby. Your tears break my heart."

And that did it. With a sob, she opened the floodgates. All those tears she'd held back for so many years burst through her emotional shields. Cord held her, touching her with gentle hands, dropping soft kisses on her hair, forehead and cheek. She'd be embarrassed when her outburst subsided, but for now she absorbed his warmth, his kindness, and accepted the fact he cared.

Jolie's sobs eventually turned to hiccups. Cord patted her back as if he wasn't sure what exactly to do. She lifted her head. When he shifted, she caught the flicker of a wince before he turned away. Despite the way he'd been moving all night, she'd bet his injuries still bothered him.

Cord offered her a smile. "Need my shirttail?"

She hiccupped again, around a little laugh, and he interrupted her before she could apologize. "Don't, sunshine."

"What? Don't blow my nose on your shirt?"

Cord laughed. "Yeah, it's okay to blow your nose on my shirt." He pressed a kiss to her forehead, and then shifted his position again. When she looked up at him, he offered a murmured, "Ah…awkward," in response.

Jolie brushed her cheek moving against his shirt. What

was she doing? He leaned and twisted, trying to see her face. She pressed her lips together, but the smile spread despite her best efforts. He glared at her. "I refuse to apologize for getting turned on around you, Jolie. I pretty much stay that way if you're anywhere within fifty feet of me." He chuckled. "Okay, to be honest, you don't even have to be in the same room. All I have to do is think about you."

She tilted her face, unsure she believed him, wanting to see his expression. She didn't speak at first, just searched his face in solemn concentration. "You really mean that, don't you?"

"Yeah. I've… Ah, hell, Jolie." He pushed away and sat up. "I'm gonna be honest here."

The debate raging inside Cord was obvious to her. Did she really want him to answer her question? She felt as if she was standing on the edge of a precipice and if she took one more step she'd fall.

No, no, no! Bad Cord. Don't do this. It's a really *bad idea. You'll ruin things. Again.* His brain wouldn't shut up so he imagined a gag. When Jolie's hand touched his shoulder, the voice in his head shut up.

"I think about you all the time, Jolie. Always have." The soft intake of her breath made him pause. Silence loomed between them until he added, "You had every right to hate me. Hell, I hated myself. Still do. I was a fool, Jolie."

"You broke my heart." Her whispered words escaped before she could stop them. He looked as if she'd ripped him into jagged pieces like a glass shattering on concrete.

"I know." He inhaled a ragged breath and combed tense fingers through his hair. "But you got your revenge. You broke mine."

Nine

Jolie balled up her fist, ready to slug Cord. How dare he make this all about him? He'd left her, shredded her heart and her self-esteem. Walked off laughing at her for being the foolish girl she was. She thought back over the things he'd revealed tonight—whether he meant to or not.

Like air hissing out of a tiny hole in a balloon, her anger leaked away.

She sat up and folded her legs tailor-style. Rubbing eyes still swollen from her crying jag, she really hoped she had no more tears left. Things were headed into unmapped emotional territory tonight. Her own feelings were hot and raw, and she desperately wanted to put off this inevitable conversation. But she'd been waiting a lot of years.

"Why, Cord?"

His shoulders hunched as he scrubbed at his face with the heels of his hands. "Short answer? My old man. He hates J. Rand. Hell, Cyrus hates just about everyone he's ever come in contact with."

His explanation felt too much like an excuse, and Jolie wasn't going to let him get by with it. "What's the long answer?"

Cord pushed off the lounger and paced toward the pool. He stood at the edge, hands shoved into his hip pockets. Jolie shivered, cool night air invading the space he'd vacated. She grabbed the chenille wrap draped nearby and tossed it around her shoulders.

"Jolie, all I ever wanted was you. That day in high school, standing there joking with Chance, Cooper and Boone? I looked up. Saw you. And damn if my world didn't come to a screeching halt." He glanced over his shoulder, saw what she'd done and moved to put another log in the fire pit. He poked until the log caught. "Then Boone told me who you were." One shoulder lifted in an apologetic shrug. "Your father's name was pretty much a nightly cussword at the Barron family dinner table. I was seventeen and our old man ruled the roost with an iron fist."

Jolie considered what she knew of Cyrus Barron but didn't speak.

"You were...beautiful. And I wanted you like I've never wanted anything in my life."

"Then why did you date so many girls?"

"I couldn't have you." He shrugged both shoulders. "That simple and that complicated. No one else compared to you. I know. I think I dated every girl in the school before I graduated. And then I started over in college. But you weren't there where I could see you every day. Where I could—" He snapped his mouth shut.

"Where you could what, Cord?" Her voice sounded soft to her own ears but somehow he heard her.

"We used to have a mimosa tree in the backyard of the house in Nichols Hills. I'd sit under that thing in the spring." He half turned away from her and stared out across the ranch. "I took a chain saw to it in college."

"I...I don't understand."

"Mimosa, Jolie. You smell like mimosa."

She barely resisted the urge to sniff her skin as the implications became apparent. "But we were dating. We were together all the time. And it was good between us. I need to know, Cord. Why did you break up with me?"

"Why did you fall into my lap at that frat party to begin with?"

"I asked you first."

"I've been answering your questions, Jolie. I think it's time you answered some of mine. Why?"

Jolie tugged the wrap tighter and considered what to say. "Easy answer? I was drunk and I had a crush on you. Had since that day in high school."

"And the hard answer?"

"Forbidden fruit." A half smile tugged the corner of her mouth. "While not a nightly topic, your family made it into conversations at my house, too." She laughed, but the sound was dry and brittle. "You know, if you'd *been* the Cord Barron everyone told me you were, I think that one night would have been the end of it. If you'd taken me to bed and said goodbye in the morning, that would have gotten you out of my system. But, oh, no. You couldn't do that. You had to be all noble and stuff. You took me back to the sorority house. You held my hair while I puked my guts up. You tucked me into bed, kissed me on the forehead and left." Tears sprang up behind her closed eyelids. "Damn you, Cord. Why couldn't you have been a jerk?"

The cushion beside her dipped, and before she could protest, Cord's arms wrapped her in their strength. He lay down and pulled her with him, cuddling her so that her head rested on his shoulder. She sniffled, but determined to continue, she added, "You made me fall in love with you and then you just…left. 'It's over,' you said. No explanation. Those two words and then you walked out the door."

"I spent the next week dead drunk." His voice grated the words.

"Why, Cord?"

"I told you, my old man. He…ah, hell, Jolie. He found out. About us. I still don't know how."

Something twisted deep inside her as Cord's words confirmed her suspicions. She curled her fingers into the placket of his shirt. "Tell me."

"He called me into his office. Made me stand there while he canted back in that big ole leather desk chair of his, hands folded across his ribs. There was a cigar burning in the ashtray and he wouldn't look at me." He gulped a couple of breaths. "When he finally looked at me…I… Dammit, Jolie, I wished he'd gotten out of his chair and decked me. It would have hurt a whole lot less than the look he gave me."

Her eyes burned and she closed them, hoping to hide the moisture threatening to spill. *No more tears*, she commanded her heart.

"I'd disappointed him, he told me. Worst son ever. All the typical BS he trots out. Every last one of us has had that manure thrown our way. But this time…this time was different. I can't say why, but it was."

Jolie rubbed her cheek against his chest, partly to smear away the tears but partly to see his expression. Cord's eyes were open, but he was staring at some spot in the redwood-planked roof above them. One hand rubbed back and forth along the curve of her hip, but she didn't think Cord was even aware of the caress. His face looked drawn and tense.

"He took me down a couple of floors, showed me the office for the CEO of BarEx. Then he said, 'Your name should be on that door, but it won't be now. You see her again, I'll strip you of your name, of your inheritance, of everything you ever dreamed of.'" Cord's voice broke on the word *dreamed*.

She stretched so she could place a gentle kiss on the point of his chin.

"I figured I could work to finish school. In the oil patch. And then go to work for just about anybody. But, oh, no. He had it all figured out. Promised I'd never work for any oil company. If I couldn't work, I couldn't have my dream."

Cord kissed the top of her head and settled her just a little bit closer with a gentle squeeze of his arm. His hand covered hers on his chest and pried her fingers from his shirt so he could lace his fingers through them. "I wanted to marry you and have a family. But I couldn't do that without a job. Or so I thought. I was young and dumb and a coward."

She opened her mouth to say that her dad would have hired him, but the words didn't come out. She thought about it. They'd been sneaking around and she had never lied to her father—until Cord. At the time, there'd been a downturn in the oil and gas business. Prices were down, the government was tightening regulations, leases were hard to come by. There would have been no way her father would hire the son of his biggest rival.

"So I ran. The night I broke up with you, Cooper drove me to the nearest liquor store and I spent about five hundred bucks. I skipped classes for a week. Coop and Chance took turns babysitting. They made sure I didn't do something stupid."

"I hated you."

"Yeah, I figured." He inhaled, held it and then exhaled slowly. "I sort of hated myself."

Neither of them spoke, and the night thickened around them. A log in the fire pit popped. Off in the distance, a mockingbird trilled a lonely warble. He spread the chenille throw out so it covered both of them.

"If you start snoring, I'm leaving."

"I don't snore, Jolie, but you do."

"Do not!" She thumped his chest with their entwined fists for emphasis.

"And you make these little mewling noises. Like a kitten." He continued to tease her.

"Liar."

"Truth."

"How would you remember that?"

"I remember everything, Jolie." His voice held no hint of teasing.

"Like what?"

"Like the way you look when you wake up. All doe eyed with your hair mussed. Like that giggle-snort thing you do when something hits your funny bone. Like the way you watch me, your eyelids half lowered, when I'm getting ready to kiss you."

"Do not."

"I'll prove it."

He pressed up from the lounge back, cradling her across his chest. She wanted to wipe the smirk off his face until he bent his head. Darn if he wasn't right—her lids drooped and she watched him from beneath her lashes. His lips touched hers and her eyes closed all on their own. She didn't fight. Her body was way past the fight-or-flight point. It was all about the shut-up-and-kiss now.

Jolie parted her lips, inviting Cord to deepen the kiss. He did. His fingers threaded in her hair and he angled her head so he could assault her mouth with heat and need. His. Hers. It no longer mattered. Her tongue danced with his, eliciting a soft groan from him. His arousal was impossible to ignore as she shifted her hips. Her core tightened, throbbing with the thought of having Cord buried there. She wanted him now as much as she ever had.

Her breasts ached, and she wished that he'd touch her there, that he'd run his thumbs over their peaks. She arched and rubbed against his chest, and thank goodness, Cord spoke her body language fluently. The hand in her hair dropped to press between her shoulder blades while his other hand cupped a breast. Air hissed from her lungs in a satisfied sigh. Her thighs tensed and she pressed her knees together as her center throbbed with need.

Then he broke the kiss. And set her away from him.

"What the—?"

"I'm sorry." Cord swung his legs off the lounger and his fists curled up on his thighs.

"Sorry? I don't understand you, Cord. What are you sorry for now?"

"For…this." He refused to look at her. "I didn't mean to…seduce you."

"Seduce? Me? Seriously?" Her burst of laughter came out more like a snort. "I think it was mutual, dude."

"No."

"I beg your pardon? I seem to remember kissing you just as hard as you were kissing me." She added, "Among other things," in an undertone.

"This isn't right, Jolie."

"What?" Totally confused, she couldn't decide if she was angry, amused or embarrassed.

"I want you. God knows I've always wanted you. But not like this."

"Uh…what does that mean?" She leaned forward and to the side so she could see part of his face. What was he up to? Was this some game he was playing?

"I just think jumping into—" With one hand, he made a vague waving gesture between them. "I want to take it slow. Do it right this time." Now he turned to face her, and the stark need on his face felt like a punch to her stomach.

"So what now?" Her voice quavered, and she prayed Cord didn't pick up on it.

"Not sure, sunshine." He cupped her cheek and leaned in to brush a gentle kiss across her lips. "I need to learn how to be a father. To CJ. We need to be friends. Not just—" He did that vague wave again.

Jolie studied his face. So many emotions congregated there she couldn't read them all.

"What do you want?"

Cord looked away, stood and put distance between them as he stared out over the pool. "Time with CJ. Well, more time with CJ. And maybe time together. As a…well, the three of us. As…friends."

He wouldn't look her in the eye, and she was positive he was planning something. "I don't trust you, Cord."

A flash of anger consumed his expression for a moment before he controlled it. "That goes both ways, Jolie."

His voice chipped at her walls like a sharp chisel. She

opened her mouth to retort, and then snapped her jaw shut. Yeah, okay. He had every right not to trust her. She'd kept the biggest secret of their lives from him.

"You're right. I'm sorry." She drew her knees up to her chest and hugged them. "This is like doing the two-step through a minefield."

"You got that right." He stepped closer, but stopped just out of her reach. "Look, can we agree that we each hurt the other? Deeply. I really do want to move forward, Jolie. I can't undo the past. I screwed up, okay? I know that. But all the apologies in the world won't change a damned thing. Here's what I want. I want the chance to make it right. To fix things."

That was the very core of Cord. He was a fixer. The classic middle child. He negotiated. Smoothed over hurt feelings. Compromised. She'd loved that about him, once upon a time. She'd watched him protect the twins and Chance from their father, but she'd also watched him surrender to Cyrus's demands. She didn't want to admit that he hadn't really changed all that much. Not in the fundamental things—an odd combination of protector and defeatist.

Though she wasn't sure she was ready to trust him, she admitted he still had way too much boyish charm to be healthy, and he oozed his way through her defenses no matter what she did to thwart him. The fact her panties were damp testified to that.

"You're insidious."

His bark of laughter echoed through the covered patio. "Don't forget incorrigible."

"You're definitely that, too. You just won't stop, and then you slime your way back into my life."

"Well, that certainly paints me in an attractive light."

"And you know what else? You're right. Sleeping with you would be a horrible idea."

He looked amused now.

"Horrible, huh?" He glanced at her chest. She knew her traitorous nipples were peaked and obvious.

Folding her arms across her chest in self-defense, she nodded emphatically. "Yes. Horrible. I momentarily lost my mind. I swear you're like one of those rainforest frogs with the poison skin. You kiss me and I lose all sense."

"I figure that's a good thing, sunshine."

Her previous thoughts returned, swamping her with misgiving. "Don't, Cord. I'm…I'm not ready for this."

"Not ready for what?" He looked cautious now.

She waved her hand between them. "This. Us. You in CJ's life. I don't trust your father, Cord. I don't trust that you'll—"

"That I'll what, Jolie?"

Now he looked angry, but she wasn't ready to reveal her thoughts, to tell him that she didn't trust him to choose her and CJ this time. She scrambled off the lounger and headed toward the door. "I'm going home."

His laughter surrounded her, so rich and warm it tasted like s'mores on her tongue, and she wavered for a moment.

"Are you sure I can't convince you to stay for the sleepover?"

"I am *not* sleeping with you, Cordell Barron. Not tonight. Not ever."

Ten

Cord reread the report. Despite any conspiracy theories to the contrary, the stuff happening on the drilling rig—including his and Cooper's injuries—appeared to be just unrelated accidents. Despite this information from Cash's investigator, Cord wasn't completely convinced. He couldn't forget how J. Rand had warned him away from Jolie at first, even though they'd declared a truce of sorts in the talk they'd had later at the ranch. And while Jolie's father wasn't nearly as cutthroat as his own, Cord couldn't completely shake the idea that the problems his company was facing were tied in somehow with Jolie's return.

He set the folder aside and stared at the drilling run reports on his desk. Though Cooper wasn't fully back on the job yet, Cord had been back in the office for about a week. But the view from his office window lured him away from work more often than not. The medical complex on the hill across town held too many memories. Bad—the pain of recovery and rehabilitation. And good—the serenity of waking up to find Jolie hovering at his bedside.

His phone buzzed and his assistant's voice informed him that Cyrus was on the line and insistent. With a grimace, he stabbed the blinking light.

"I'm busy."

"So am I. Did you really think you could hide it from me?"

Cord did *not* want to have this conversation. "Hide what?"

"Your bastard."

Anger and adrenaline surged through him, making him reckless. "You mean my *son*?"

"Not until you file the paperwork, Cordell. Do it. Now. Or I will."

The old man hung up before Cord could retort. His day had just turned into a big whole heaping pile of dog crap.

Business. He had to focus on BarEx. His private life was screwed at the moment even though he'd managed to work out a schedule of sorts with Jolie, giving him time with CJ—but not time with her. He was still kicking himself for calling a halt to their lovemaking that night. And now his old man knew about CJ. "You are all kinds of a fool, son," he muttered.

"So what else is new?"

He whipped around, surprised he hadn't heard the door open. "Damn, Chance. Give me a heart attack next time."

His brother laughed and dropped into a guest chair, legs stretched toward Cord's desk, booted feet crossed at the ankle as he made himself at home. "Glad to see you back."

"And that's reason enough to sneak up on me?"

"Nope. I'm here at Cassie's behest."

"And?"

"She's thinking about Thanksgiving."

"Thanksgiving." Cord repeated the word, his thoughts still on the conversation he'd just had with Cyrus—a conversation he wasn't ready to share with Chance.

"Yeah. I know. It's September and state fair time but she's already planning for the holidays."

The Great State Fair of Oklahoma. All sorts of possibilities ran through his head. Cord grinned and mentally rubbed his hands together. Perfect. He'd call Jolie, invite her and CJ. He'd run out of time. He had to convince Jolie they belonged together.

"Earth to Cord."

"Wha—? Oh. Tell Cassie whatever."

"I see the wheels turning, bro. What are you up to?"

"Nothing to do with Cassie, I assure you."

Chance rolled his eyes and laughed. "Yeah, I figured that. Let's firm up Thanksgiving, and then you can fill me in on whatever nefarious plan you're cooking up. Cassie wants to do a big family dinner at the ranch."

"Yours or ours?"

"The Crown B. We'll be lucky if our house is ready by Christmas."

Chance and Cassie were building a new home on the Crazy M, the ranch she'd inherited and saved from the old man's machinations. "Why the hell would Cassie want to do it at the B?"

"I keep asking her that and she just rolls her eyes." Chance shrugged. "I think it has to do with the fact that we consider the ranch home. Cass is all about family and home now."

"What about her and the old man?"

Chance leaned his head back and laughed. "My wife is fearless, and I quote, 'Let that sorry old bastard do his worst. I'm not afraid of him. The ranch is your family's home and that's what Thanksgiving is all about.'"

"Well, all righty, then. Cass scares me sometimes, bro."

"Yeah, you and me both. But I don't foresee any problems unless she and Miz Beth fight over the kitchen."

"Does the old man know about this crazy plan of hers?"

"Yeah, about that? I don't think so. Cass isn't worried. And frankly? Watching my wife tear into our father is worth the price of admission." Chance's gaze shifted so he was no longer looking directly at Cord.

He waited, knowing there was more to come. "What?"

Chance's smile disappeared. "She wants to invite CJ. And Jolie."

"Ah. That could be a problem if it's a *real* family event. If the old man is around—" Cord snapped his jaw shut and inhaled several times. "That would *not* be a good idea."

His hand dropped on top of the file and he drummed his fingers on it as he stared at his brother. "Have you seen the notes from the investigation Cash ran on the accident?"

"Changing the subject, big bro?"

Cord lifted one shoulder in a negligent shrug. He wasn't quite ready to get personal yet. He needed to work, focus on what he did best—find oil and natural gas, tap it and get it to a Barron refinery. "Business, Chance."

"I got a copy of the report. What about the tool pusher? Is he sloppy?"

"I don't buy it. Cooper has complete faith in the man. And Cash's guy couldn't find any signs of sabotage."

"I hear a *but* in there, Cord."

"Just seems a bit coincidental. J. Rand warns me away from Jolie, and then the well on the lease we outbid him on suddenly develops problems? I don't believe in coincidences."

"What's the pusher's safety record?"

Cord tapped the folder again. "Impeccable." He swiveled in his chair and stared at the hospital complex on the hill. He heard Chance shift in his chair and the sounds of rustling paper. "Thanksgiving isn't the only reason you came. What's up?"

"Did you look over the proposal on the Houston refinery?"

He swiveled back around and resisted the urge to roll his eyes. "Yes. And the old man seems to have covered all the bases despite my lack of input." Something in his brother's expression made him lean closer. "What? There's something in the deal you don't like?"

"Cyrus wants to set up a shell corporation for the refinery."

"For tax purposes?"

"Ostensibly."

"I hear a *but* in there, too, bro."

"He wants the shell separate from the family trust."

Cord considered the implications, and then rubbed his forehead to smooth away the furrows that thinking created. "He wants control of it. Just him."

"That's my thought." Chance shifted uncomfortably. "You're still CEO, Cord. The sale doesn't go through without your signature, despite what the old man says."

Cord ran his fingers through his hair, glad it was finally growing out from where it had been cut in the hospital. "We need the refinery, Chance. I'll go through the file, make some calls. Anything else?"

Chance pushed to his feet and turned toward the door. He hesitated and glanced over his shoulder. "Maybe the problems are a little closer to home, Cord. The old man is still pissed that I outsmarted him on the family trust."

Or it was a way to control Cord. Again. Chance left, shutting the door behind him, leaving Cord with far too much to think about.

Jolie slipped her cell phone into her pocket as Liza, the on-duty flight nurse, pulled up a chair and got comfortable by propping her feet on Jolie's desk. "You look as if you just bit into a lemon. Man trouble?"

Trying her best not to sigh, Jolie shook her head. "No. Yes... Sort of."

Her friend laughed. "Well, which is it?"

"It's Cord." As if that explained everything. To Jolie, it did.

"Honey, he's good-looking, employed, rich and he dotes on your kid. I don't see this as trouble."

"You'd be surprised," Jolie muttered darkly. "He just called asking to take CJ and me to the state fair."

"Wait. The dude is a Barron. He could fly you to freaking Paris for dinner and he wants to take you to the state freaking fair? Hon, you *do* have man trouble!"

Liza's expression was so comical, Jolie had to laugh.

"No, he called to see if he could take CJ, and then included me in the invitation."

"Wait. Asking you was an afterthought? What's wrong with the guy?"

"Liza, you do realize that Cord is CJ's father, right? We…have a history."

The nurse's boots hit the floor with a thud as she came straight up in her chair. "Wait, what? Cordell Barron is your baby daddy? Holy cannoli, woman! That is some history."

"I don't exactly tell everyone."

"I'm not everyone. I'm like your new best friend. I should know these things. But more important, at least to me, is there more like him at home? 'Oh, wait, why, yes, Liza, my new best friend in the whole wide world, there *are* three more Barrons at home and I'd love to fix you up on a double date.'"

Jolie snorted and the swig of coffee she'd just taken exited her nose. Coughing and laughing, she mopped up the mess while she caught her breath. When she could speak again, she shook a finger at Liza. "Trust me. You do not want to be anywhere near the Barron brothers."

"Trust me, yes, I do! Rich, handsome and single. What's not to love?" Liza winked and nudged Jolie's chair with her foot. "So talk to me, woman."

"There's not much to talk about. Cord and I used to date. Then we didn't. Then we sort of had a drive-by date and… nine months later, CJ popped out." She refused to look directly at Liza, preferring to straighten a desk already so neat it would make an OCD sufferer proud.

Liza gave her the stink eye and Jolie could picture the wheels turning in the other woman's head. She knew the moment Liza figured it out. "Oh. Em. Gee, Jolie. He didn't know. Damn, girl. Why would you not tell him?"

Jolie wished the heat flooding her cheeks would go away. Liza had her pegged dead to rights. "That's a really long story—one far too reminiscent of Romeo and Juliet to make me comfortable. Plus, there was that whole we'd-broken-up thing. And it was just a one-night stand. The thing is, he knows now and wants to make up for lost time."

"Again, this is a problem *why*?" Liza stared so long and hard, Jolie had to look away first. "You still care about him. Honey, this isn't a problem. Why not go out with him? See if the sparks are still there."

"Sparks? It's more like a forest fire." Jolie ripped the alligator clip from her hair and combed her fingers through the tangled mass before twisting it back up and reattaching the clip. "The man drives me crazy."

"So go with him and CJ to the fair. Drive *him* crazy for a change."

Liza's suggestion made sense, but for one thing. He'd asked to take CJ, and then included her as an afterthought. Besides, her ego still stung that he'd stopped short of making love to her when she'd all but thrown herself at him.

"I'll see." Not much of an answer, but it was the only one she currently had.

Cord stared at his son as CJ danced impatiently in front of him. The kid had insisted on going on every ride he was tall enough for, and dragged Cord along because he didn't want to ride alone. He'd held out hope that Jolie would change her mind at the last minute and come with them but she'd insisted he and CJ needed bonding time—just the two of them.

Cord had finally steered CJ away from the midway, but then the kid grazed his way down the food row. Deep-fried cupcakes. Deep-fried watermelon. Funnel cakes. Hot dogs—deep-fried with chili. Cotton candy. Fresh-squeezed lemonade. A suicide snow cone.

"Dang, bubba. Where are you puttin' it all?"

"Uh-oh. Is dang a swear jar word?"

"Nope. *Dang* is safe. But seriously, CJ. Haven't you had enough to eat?"

"Nuh-uh. One more, Daddy. 'Kay?" CJ tugged him down the row of food-vendor trailers. He stopped in front of a place advertising deep-fried strawberry shortcakes. "Please, Dad? I want one. I promise I won't eat anything else. Please? Please, please, please."

Hiding his grimace, Cord stepped to the window and ordered. When the food arrived, he walked CJ over to a picnic table and made the boy sit before putting the treat and a handful of napkins in front of him.

"Want a bite, Daddy?"

"Ah…no." Cord did his best not to look askance at the glob on CJ's spoon. He liked deep-fried food as much as the next red-blooded American male but some things were just *not* meant to be dipped in batter and fried.

CJ inhaled his dessert, declared he was thirsty and pouted briefly when Cord insisted he drink a bottle of water.

By the time CJ was done, the midway was shutting down. The little boy was dead on his feet as they walked toward the parking lot. Halfway there, Cord picked him up and carried him. Despite walking all over the fair, Cord felt remarkably fit.

CJ was all but asleep by the time they reached Cord's sleek little sports car. He buckled his son into his car seat, and a few minutes later, they were headed across town to Cord's condo in Bricktown.

He was happy to be home again. Once his physical therapist had cleared him and he'd started back to work, the commute from the ranch was a pain—not to mention he wanted his own space. Of course, he'd worked his butt off in PT to get out of the damn wheelchair and then to get rid of the walker.

Waking up when Cord unbuckled him, CJ groaned. "I want Mommy," he whined. "My tummy hurts."

Cord picked up the boy in a reverse piggyback across

his chest. "I'll call her as soon as we get upstairs, bubba. Just hang in—"

Something hot and wet splattered down Cord's back. He barely set CJ down before the next wave of vomiting hit. He went to grab his cell phone, but stopped when he realized the thing was in his hip pocket—the pocket covered with deep-fried something.

Thankfully, he had a private entrance on the ground floor. He got CJ inside, undressed him and laid him down on the couch with an ice pack, a wet washcloth and a plastic bucket.

Stripping out of his clothes with the utmost care, Cord donned a pair of rubber gloves he found in the supply closet and fished the important stuff out of his pockets. Luckily, his phone didn't seem any worse for the wear. He dialed Jolie's number just as CJ called for him. He got back to the living room barely in time to hold the bucket.

"Cord?" Jolie's voice echoed from the other end of the line.

He wiped CJ's mouth and snagged his phone. "Jolie? Thank God. Can you come over?"

"What's—?"

"Is that Mommy? I want Mommy." CJ raised his voice. "Mommy? My tummy hurts and I upchucked."

"Cord, what in the world is going on?"

"We're at my condo. Can you come? I'd come to you but… Hold on."

After he dealt with another round of sickness, he grabbed the phone again. "CJ's—"

"I can hear, Cord. I'm on my way."

By the time the doorbell rang fifteen minutes later, CJ had been able to hold down a few sips of ginger ale and was dozing on the couch. Cord realized he was wearing nothing but his socks and boxers only after he opened the door to Jolie's arched eyebrow.

"Let me guess, you haven't done laundry and you had nothing else to wear."

"Well…" Cord scratched his chest. "Actually, I threw the clothes we were wearing in the washer but I haven't started the cycle yet. I've been a little busy."

"I can imagine." Jolie stared at his chest—was that a look of hunger in her eyes? At his suggestive chuckle, she dragged her gaze back to his face. "How is he?"

"Better, I think. He had some ginger ale and is asleep."

"See, you can handle it. Not sure why I'm here."

"Because he wanted you?" There was no rancor in his voice. He remembered being sick as a kid and wanting his mom—his real one or Helen, the second Mrs. Barron. Too bad neither of them had survived to see the Barron boys grow up.

He offered what he hoped was a winning smile. "C'mon in. I'll go grab some jeans."

Cord insisted Jolie precede him. No sense letting her see just how much she affected him—which was all too evident by the activity in his boxers.

He grabbed a clean pair of jeans from the dryer, started the washer and headed back to the living room.

"Can I get you something to—?"

"Rule number one, Cord."

He stopped dead in his tracks as she held up one finger. Remaining silent, he simply arched a brow.

"Little boys do not need to eat everything in sight."

"Yeah, I sorta figured that out."

"Rule number two." She added a second finger. "Little boys will beg to eat everything in sight. Refer back to rule number one." The way she enunciated the last three words made Cord want to laugh.

He worked on his expression so he could appear chagrined rather than amused. Hoping boyish charm would help, he said, "I'm sorry, Jolie. This is all sort of new to me, y'know?"

Her face clouded up and he once again held up his hands, palm out, in hopes of placating her. "Whoa, sunshine. I was simply stating a fact, not casting blame. Okay?"

Jolie huffed out a breath that ruffled her bangs and nodded. "Okay."

He tried another dose of charm by way of a crooked grin as he pressed his suit. "And you know, we could have avoided this whole situation if you'd just come with us."

She glared at him but he caught the twinkle in her eye. "Oh, so this is *my* fault?"

"Why don't I get you something to drink while we figure out who's at fault?"

Jolie followed him into the kitchen. "Don't think for one minute that your charm will get you out of this one, Cord Barron." She narrowed her gaze and all but shook her finger at him.

"Ah, so you admit I'm charming." He flashed another grin and waggled his brows at her before ducking behind the refrigerator door. Cord bit back his laughter at her exasperated huff. He emerged with a pitcher of tea and fixed her a tall glass with ice from the freezer door. As he watched her take a sip, the tightness in his chest eased—and the tightness farther south ramped up a little. He'd gotten the sweetness in the tea right, judging by the look on her face, but seeing her swallow put all sorts of thoughts in his head, thoughts he throttled given their son slept on the couch in the next room.

He offered her a chair at the kitchen table, sitting once she'd settled. "I'm sorry, sunshine. I told you I need to learn to be a dad. Those self-help books don't help at all."

She choked back a quick laugh, but her gaze softened as she regarded him. Progress. "I should have warned you but there's no better teacher than experience."

Unable to resist the urge, he touched the back of her hand, and then ran his fingertip up her arm. Goose bumps.

Yeah, he liked that he could still affect her like that. "Thanks for coming when I called."

"You're welcome. I suppose I should get him home."

"Do you have to go?"

She gazed at him and he didn't flinch. There'd been too much secrecy between them. He wanted everything out in the open. Ever since their talk at the ranch, when he'd barely stopped from making love to her, he'd been wearing down her defenses. He wanted her in the worst way, but he wanted to do it right this time. He wanted to build a real relationship—one based on trust and friendship as well as the heat they generated. Chemistry made for great sex, but it took more to make a relationship. And he wanted a relationship with Jolie, one beyond the fact she was the mother of his child. The time for hesitation was over.

"Go out with me, Jolie."

"What?"

"Go out with me. A date. Dinner."

"I don't think that's a good idea."

"I think it's an excellent idea. I'm not ashamed of CJ, Jolie. Or you."

"What about your father?"

"Let me worry about Cyrus. Frankly, I'm more worried about yours."

"Dad?" Confusion filtered into her expression. "Why would you worry about Dad?"

"He warned me away from you. Last summer."

"It obviously didn't work."

"Nope. It sure didn't. So? Dinner?"

Eleven

Mrs. Corcoran, the nanny, answered the door, and Cord did his best not to fidget under her intense gaze. A week had passed since the state fair fiasco, but from the way the woman glared, Jolie had told her all about it. As she continued to stare, he brushed past her and surreptitiously checked his fly to make sure it was zipped.

"Daddy!" CJ flew at him, and Cord braced for his son's leap into his arms. His ribs only pulled a little.

"Hey, bubba!"

"Mommy'll be down in a minute. She's gettin' pretty. Where you gonna take her? How come I can't go? When will you—?"

"Whoa, CJ. One question at a time. I'm taking your mom out to dinner at a really fancy restaurant. You can't go because this is a grown-up date and you don't like escargot."

"Easy car go? What's that?"

"*Escargot* is the French word for snails."

"Eww. You're gonna eat snails?"

"Nope. Not me, but your mom likes the little suckers."

"I do like them." Jolie had crept up behind them, and she gave CJ a teasing pinch on his side, making the little boy giggle as he arched away from her.

"Wow. You look…beautiful."

"Gee, thanks, Cord. Don't sound so surprised."

He couldn't tell from Jolie's wry expression if she was upset, which would be weird because she did look beautiful. Something about her tone of voice finally clicked the lightbulb on. "Oh. Oh! No, no. I didn't mean it like that. I'm not surprised, I'm… Wow." He winked at CJ. "Bubba, you have the most beautiful mom in the entire world and I'm the lucky man who gets to take her out to dinner tonight." He set the boy down and turned to Mrs. Corcoran. "We won't be out too late."

"CJ and I will be just fine. Go have a good time."

The restaurant atop the Founders Tower had been known by many different names during its years of operation. Like the famous Space Needle in Seattle, the outer rim of the restaurant slowly spun around the central tower, offering up the full vista of Oklahoma City. The center held the reception area, elevators, bar, dance floor and kitchens.

As they headed to the top floor, people in the crowded elevator remained silent. Canned music filtered through a tinny speaker as everyone stared straight ahead. Jolie hated elevators, not that she was claustrophobic or anything. She leaned closer to Cord, and when he took her hand, she cut her eyes to gauge his expression. He, too, was staring straight ahead, but the dimple on his right cheek was peeking out at her.

His profile—heck, his whole face—never failed to make her heart skip a beat. All the Barron boys had been blessed, and they each bore the distinctive stamp of their DNA, as evidenced by Cassie Barron's immediately recognizing CJ as being one of the clan. They were handsome, but Cord had something more. Laugh lines feathered around golden-brown eyes that glinted with mischief. Sculpted cheekbones, jaw and nose. The man could pose for a Greek statue.

While his features would make any girl look twice, it had always been his personality that kept Jolie's interest. He was funny, wise and ornery—often at the same time.

He squeezed her hand and pulled it up to his mouth.

After placing a soft kiss on the back of her hand, he glanced down and winked.

If she didn't stay on guard, Cord could steamroll right over her emotions. *And what's wrong with that?* She wanted to swat the annoying inner voice whispering in her ear every time the subject of Cord came up.

The elevator doors slid open and the passengers surged forward. Cord held back until the crowd cleared out, and then escorted Jolie off. The maître d's gaze landed on them almost immediately.

"Mr. Barron. Good evening, sir. Right this way. Your table is ready."

Those waiting to be seated parted like the Red Sea, but as the crowd closed back in behind her, Jolie heard the whispers start. While some of those murmurs were from diners upset that she and Cord were seated immediately, others were about Cord. Stories on the Barrons often appeared in the media.

The maître d' paused on the edge of the dance floor, waiting as tables slowly passed by. A moment later, their table arrived, and he cautioned them to be careful as they stepped onto the revolving section.

Once they were seated, Cord ordered champagne before opening his menu and commenting, "They've completely renovated the restaurant and updated the mechanics so this part rotates again."

"I remember coming here with Dad when I was a little girl."

They reminisced over memories of their childhoods and how many near misses they'd had in meeting before that fateful day in high school. Jolie fought to smother her laughter as Cord inhaled his steak. She managed to get through her lobster without wearing it. The table they shared was narrow, and every time she shifted in her very comfortable chair, her foot or leg or knee grazed Cord's. He pretended to ignore the contact just as she did—*pretend* being the operative word. Each touch revved up her heart rate and reminded her of the feel of his body pressed against hers.

She'd look up at odd moments to catch him watching her, something hot and sexy in his gaze, as if she was every bit as delicious as that steak as he was savoring. Jolie would get fascinated by his mouth, his lips, and she really wanted to taste them.

"Are you finished, Jolie?"

She jerked her gaze to his eyes—the ones twinkling even as his mouth curved up in that irritating grin of his. The waiter stood patiently, holding Cord's plate.

"Oh. Yes. I am. Thank you."

The man whisked her plate away and handed both sets of dishes off to a hovering busboy. "Will you be enjoying dessert tonight?"

Jolie knew what she'd like to have for dessert, and by the way Cord was looking at her, he was imagining her covered in chocolate and whipped cream. Just to tease him, she ordered cheesecake.

While they waited for dessert, Cord stood, took her hand and walked her onto the dance floor. A small combo was playing live music, and he took her into his arms for a slow dance. His cologne, something brisk and citrusy, caused her to inhale deeply. The music changed, and without missing a beat, Cord led her in a passable samba.

"I didn't know you could dance."

"Mmm. There's a lot of things you don't know about me. Personally, I'd rather be doing a two-step at Toby Keith's, but this'll do for now." His lips brushed across her forehead a moment before he stopped dancing and escorted her back to their table for dessert.

As she spooned the rich caramel cheesecake into her mouth, Jolie couldn't decide which was more decadent—the creamy treat or the man sitting across from her watching through hooded lids as she took each bite.

She resisted scraping the plate to get the last bit before she finished the ice wine Cord had ordered with dessert. He looked as if he wanted to lick her the same way she'd been licking her spoon. Blushing, she watched him from the relative safety of a tilted glance.

"So what's next on the menu?" she asked.

His dimple played peekaboo with the upturned corner of his mouth, and Jolie suddenly realized why heroines in romance novels swooned.

"What if I said *you*?"

She wanted to fan her face. And other places, warmer and damper. For a brief instant, Jolie considered knocking a glass of ice water into her lap. With her luck, steam would rise and Cord would know exactly what she was thinking. She knew better than to answer. Any reply would come out a squeak.

His gaze heated and focused on her mouth. Raking her teeth across her bottom lip, she was gratified to see his irises dilate. He was as turned on as she was. But this was their first official, grown-up date. Falling into bed with him—no matter how badly she wanted to do just that— would set a dangerous precedent for the rest of their relationship. However things worked out between them.

"C'mon." He pushed back from the table, stood and held out his hand to her.

Placing her hand in his was a leap of faith on her part. He pulled her to her feet, tucked her hand into the crook of his elbow and guided her across the dance floor toward the exit. He said nothing in the elevator, nothing as they waited for the valet to return with Cord's car. He remained silent as he handed her into the passenger seat and settled behind the wheel. Then they were off. Problem was she had no clue where they were headed and Cord still wasn't talking.

He passed the exit that would take her home, which made sense once she thought it over. CJ was at home. And Mrs. Corcoran. She didn't want an audience. When he headed into the heart of Bricktown, she pressed her knees together. His condo. Except he passed the street where it was located. A few minutes later, he pulled up in front of the newest club in the downtown entertainment district.

A valet opened her door and she slid out, a question on her lips as Cord came around the back of the car to meet her.

"I hope you don't mind mixing a little business with our pleasure."

Jolie quirked a brow. "I'm not sure I understand."

"Live band. Chase asked me to give them a look."

"Oh. Is he still in Vegas?"

"No. He's in Nashville at the moment. He's expanding, taking Barron Entertainment into the music business. Chance is tone-deaf and only listens to country music. Cash is out of town. That means I drew the short straw."

Before she could question him further, two muscular men waved them past the waiting line and opened the front doors. A wave of sound crashed over her as she entered. She would have turned around and run if Cord's hand hadn't landed on the small of her back, urging her forward.

He found an empty table with tall stools near the bar. A harried waitress paused long enough for Cord to whisper in her ear. The next thing he did surprised Jolie. He handed her a set of earplugs. She stared at the orange lumps in the palm of his hand, and then glanced up. He grinned and winked as he fitted a second set into his own ears with his other hand.

After she'd stuffed the spongy plugs in, the noise level dropped to almost acceptable levels. The waitress returned with a scotch on the rocks for Cord and a frozen margarita, extra salt, for Jolie. The man never forgot a thing. She needed to remember that.

The musicians provided a driving beat and Cord offered her a dance. When they returned to the table, a group of rowdy men had taken up residence at the next table. The two facing her looked her up and down, their interest obvious.

"Will you look at that? That is one hot-damn bitchin' woman, fellas."

The other two turned to look. One grabbed his crotch and rubbed. "I'd sure like to nail me some of that."

Despite the loud music and earplugs, their obnoxious comments filtered across her consciousness. Cord stiffened beside her. He hadn't missed the lewd suggestions, either. All four men were obviously inebriated. And Cord wasn't 100 percent recovered from his injuries, despite his assurances to the contrary. Four against one weren't good odds on his best day. She put her hand on his arm as he stood up.

"Let it go. They're drunk jerks."

He ignored her and she sighed. Testosterone drained a man's brain of all common sense. Cord kissed her cheek, but it felt too much like a pat on the head for comfort. *Here*, he seemed to say with the gesture. *Big bad caveman will take care of his little woman.*

She couldn't hear what he said to the men, but the biggest guy in the group jumped up, knocking his stool over. In the blink of an eye, he was swinging on Cord, who ducked under the blow and came up with a fist to the guy's gut. The other three jumped into the fray. Fists and elbows flew—the four jerks landing blows on each other as often as they managed to punch Cord. By the time the muscular bouncers arrived, Cord had gotten more than a few licks in, to good effect. Two of the men were on the floor unconscious and Cord was holding his own with the other two. The bouncers separated the men, and with the help of a couple of additional security types, all of them were bundled off to the back of the club.

Jolie followed, not quite sure what else to do. The bouncer standing watch wouldn't let her into the secured area, so she waited in the hallway as the police arrived. She paced and fidgeted as the fire department and then EMTs appeared. Had Cord been hurt? Panicked, she pushed past the man standing guard at the door. He had his arm around her waist attempting to subdue her when Cord's voice cut through the hubbub in the office.

"You will take your hands off her now."

The guy dropped her as if she had girl cooties. "Cord? Are you okay? What's going on?"

One of the cops turned to give her an appraising once-over. Cord growled, and that was when she realized he was in handcuffs. "Wha-what's going on? You aren't arresting him, are you? That's not fair. They jumped him."

"We're taking them all in, ma'am."

"Jolie, my keys are in my pocket, along with my phone. I'm sorry, sunshine. Call Chance and then drive yourself home."

The police allowed her to get his keys and cell and then hustled the men—all cuffed—out the back door of the club. The club's chief of security touched her shoulder. "Miss Davis? I'll escort you out front and have Mr. Barron's car brought around for you."

As she waited for the car, she called Chance, filled him in and asked where to meet him. Ten minutes later, she was parked in front of the county jail building. Chance wouldn't be there for at least thirty minutes. She called Mrs. Corcoran, told the woman she'd be late and settled in to wait.

A tap on the window brought her up out of an uneasy doze with a start. Sharp pain lanced through her neck and her pulse was racing. Chance and Cord stood next to the car. Chance looked amused. Cord looked as if he'd gone nine rounds with a heavyweight boxer.

She climbed out of the car, Cord's injuries her immediate concern. "I need to take you to the ER."

"Sunshine, I'm fine."

Jolie glanced at Chance, who nodded. "EMTs checked him over. Nothing needs stitching, no broken bones. He just needs ibuprofen and ice."

She blew out a breath, and while she really wanted to chew Cord a new one, she was relieved he wasn't seriously hurt. Still, she wanted to check for herself—not that she didn't trust the EMTs, but… "Get in. I'll drive you home."

Cord was dozing, head braced against the passenger window, when Jolie pulled into her driveway. She'd driven to her home instinctively. Thinking discretion was the better part of having to explain her evening, Jolie left Cord sleeping in the car while she made sure CJ and his nanny were both asleep.

Getting Cord out of the car and inside her house was another matter. He was stiff and sore, and no matter where she touched him, he winced. Without conscious thought on her part, he ended up sprawled across her king-size bed. Her bedroom was on the first floor, the guest room on the second. That was the excuse her libido kept giving her conscience.

Grabbing as many frozen gel packs as she had in her freezer, Jolie returned to her room.

"Hey." Why did she feel so shy?

"I'm sorry."

Cord's apology stopped her midstep. "Sorry?"

"Yeah. Not exactly the way I wanted this date to end." He patted the bed beside him. "Come keep me company while you slap those cold puppies on me." He moved to scoot over to make room and winced. "Damn. I hurt everywhere."

She positioned the cold packs on his injuries before ducking into her bathroom to rummage for pain meds and a glass of water. After he swallowed the pills, she settled on the edge of the bed.

"You always were a white knight, Cord, but trust me when I say tonight wasn't worth you getting the crap beat out of you just because those jerks were mouthy." She worried when he closed his eyes and blanched. His brow furrowed in pain. "I wish there was something more I could do."

One corner of his mouth quirked, pulling at the split in his lip. "Oww." He didn't open his eyes as he added, "You could kiss it and make it better."

Twelve

Cord peeked through one eye to see what Jolie's response would be. She rolled her eyes and snorted. Not what he was hoping for, but better than a slap.

"I don't think there's one spot on your entire body that isn't beat-up. I don't want to hurt you."

He opened both eyes and studied her expression. "Sunshine, there's no way you could hurt me." Not physically anyway. She'd already pretty much laid his heart bare, but the more time he spent with her, and with CJ, the quicker that pain receded from memory.

With a sassy smirk, she dropped a kiss just above his swollen eye. "Does this hurt?"

"A little. Maybe kiss me here?" He pointed to the corner of his mouth. She leaned in and carefully placed a kiss there. Fighting the urge to turn his head and take her kiss full on the mouth, he waited until she straightened. Next, he pointed to a spot on the side of his throat. "Doesn't hurt here."

She again bent and nuzzled him. Oh, damn, but that felt good. Little spasms of electricity danced all the way to his groin, and things stirred down there in response.

"Uh…how 'bout here?" He managed to unbutton his shirt and pointed to his chest.

Jolie trailed her fingers through the dark hair sprouting there and made a funny noise in the back of her throat. Oh, yeah. He liked the sound of that. Before he could encourage her any more, CJ's voice echoed from a monitor on the nightstand beside them.

"Mommy?"

Jolie pushed to her feet. "I'll be right back."

Cord took advantage of her absence. Rolling off the bed, he kicked off his boots and headed to the bathroom. He washed his face and hands, assessing his injuries in the mirror. He looked like something the cat dragged in, ate and spat out as a hairball. And felt worse. Stripping out of his ripped dress shirt, he padded back to the bedroom.

Jolie stood in the doorway, staring. He arched a brow.

"Is there any part of you that's not black-and-blue?"

He glanced at the floor and chuckled. "The soles of my feet?"

"You're nuts, Cord. You know that, right?"

Yes, he knew. He was nuts about her. Nuts for ever walking away. And maybe he was nuts for trying to convince her to let him back into her life.

"I don't know how you do it." The words tumbled out before he could think about them.

"How I do what?"

"Be a mom." When she bristled, he held up a hand to keep the peace. "A single mom. I mean, I know you have help. But damn, honey. It's hard work."

Jolie took half a step back, almost as if she'd taken a blow. This conversation wasn't going the way he'd played it out in his head.

"Wow. I don't think I ever expected to hear something like that from you."

He walked closer, but she looked so nervous he stopped at the foot of the bed. "Why didn't you tell me? I would have married you, you know."

And damn if that wasn't what he meant to say, too. He needed to get his brain in gear and find a muzzle, ASAP.

She flushed and crossed her arms over her chest. After

several tries, she choked out, "I didn't want you because of your misplaced sense of duty."

"I don't think that's it." Her eyes narrowed, but this time his brain was agile enough to keep his foot out of his mouth. "It's because I'd already left you once, right? You didn't want to take the chance I'd do it again." He swallowed his anger and tunneled his fingers through his hair. "I don't want to fight, sunshine. I screwed up. Royally. I know that. I'm sorry."

Her expression softened. "I'm sorry, too, Cord."

He inhaled several times while he marshaled his thoughts, and an idea that had niggled at him for some time finally solidified. "Don't you get it?"

Jolie's face scrunched up into that inscrutable expression indicating she didn't. "Obviously not."

Convinced he was on to something, he blurted out, "If you'd told me, it would have been our way out. Hell, if I'd been smart enough to think it through, I'd have gotten you pregnant in college."

Her mouth opened and closed a few times, and he had to fight the urge to grab her and kiss her until she connected the dots.

"Honey, we would have gotten married. You being pregnant? That would have been the one reason the old man couldn't stop us from being together."

"What?" Her voice rose in a screech and her face flushed, the pink coming all the way up her chest and neck to stain her cheeks. "Of all the stupid, idiotic…insane things to say to me, Cord Barron."

He offered the grin that always made her eyes go soft, and they did, right on schedule. "Think about it. A story about Cyrus Barron having an illegitimate grandson hitting the media? He'd be screaming defamation and slander. My old man wouldn't have liked it, but he wouldn't have fought us."

Of course, the rumor of his father having a few chil-

dren born on the wrong side of the blanket had never fazed
the sorry SOB—not that any of his legitimate sons could
officially prove they had half siblings out there—Kaden
Waite's family resemblance notwithstanding. They'd never
broached the subject with Kaden, but none of his brothers
would object if he wanted to have a DNA test done.

Jolie took a step toward him. Then another. Suddenly,
she was running. Cord braced himself, but she stopped
right in front of him. She was so close, and he wanted her
in his arms. Wrapping them around her, Cord toppled backward onto the bed, bringing her with him. He just managed
to hide his grimace as pain lanced through his entire body.

Cupping his face in her palms, Jolie attempted to keep
her weight off him. Her face hovered inches from his and
he did his best not to look at her cross-eyed.

"Oh, you beautiful, impossible man."

Was she complaining or was that somehow a compli-
ment? She kissed him, so he took it as a good thing.

"I never wanted to leave you, Jolie. I was stupid. And
a coward and—"

"Shut up, Cord." She kissed him again, gentler this time
as she remembered his injuries. "Make love to me."

One part of his brain wondered how he would manage
that with her on top and in charge—and him beat all to hell.
Then another part perked right up and muttered something
about letting Jolie be in charge. Not to be left out, his heart
spoke up, making sure to be heard when he spoke out loud.

"Always, Jolie. I always want to make love to you."

She reared back, staring down at him with a little V
forming between her brows. "That's how you feel? It wasn't
just sex?"

"Caring about you. Wanting you. I have since the moment I looked up and saw you at the top of those stairs."

As her eyes went all gooey, his libido fist pumped. He'd
found the perfect thing to say. His conscience twinged a
little, but he mentally told it to shut up. He *had* loved her

from that moment on—at least as much as he understood love. He'd wanted her, and once their relationship started in college, she'd made him feel things he hadn't felt before. Wasn't that love? He was stupid for letting her get away—something he fully planned to rectify from this moment forward.

Jolie reached to turn off the bedside lamp, and he stopped her with a gentle hand on her arm. "I want to see you, Jolie, want to watch you when you come."

"I… I'm not that wide-eyed girl anymore, Cord."

She blushed. The girl who had all but seduced him in the party room of his fraternity house had gotten shy? "Jolie?"

The pink flushing her skin turned crimson. She started to climb off him. "This is a dumb—"

He wrapped an arm around her, keeping her in place. "No, sunshine. You aren't that girl. You're so much more. You're a beautiful woman. You're the mother of my—"

She jerked away again. He let her go, and then sat up on the edge of the bed. "Jolie, come here." She complied. Reluctantly. He stood and turned her around with gentle hands on her shoulders. Unzipping her dress, he brushed it off her shoulders, letting it slide down her body to puddle at her feet. He walked around her, pausing to kiss her before he looked his fill.

Her breasts were plumper than he remembered, her hips wider. She'd blossomed from a slim girl into lush womanhood. He inhaled sharply, the front of his slacks tenting. "Damn but you're beautiful, baby."

Jolie shook her head, refusing to look at him. He grabbed her hand and pressed it to his erection. "If you don't believe my words, believe this. I may be beat to hell and back, but I want you. So. Damn. Much."

She jerked her hand back and he let it go. Her arms folded across her abdomen, but he pulled them away and sank to his knees, kissing her tummy.

"Don't." The word came out strangled.

"Why not, Jolie? What are you afraid of? What don't you want me to see?"

Her hands fluttered across her skin, and then he saw the fine feathering of white lines. Stretch marks. From her pregnancy. He kissed a trail along one of the lines. "These are beautiful."

"Yeah, and you're crazy."

"Been called that before, but they are, Jolie. You're beautiful." His palm cupped the rounded pooch of her tummy. "My son was here. Growing. Damn, woman, there's nothing sexier than that."

"Your *son*? I suppose if I'd had a little girl, that wouldn't be sexy at all."

She spit the words, but he deflected them with a smile as he rose. "A baby girl. Now, there's a thought to give a man a heart attack." His eyes twinkled as he nuzzled his way across her breasts to kiss the soft skin under her chin. "I don't think there would have been enough shotguns in the world to keep the boys at bay if we'd had a daughter."

He cupped her cheeks and kissed her, his tongue teasing the seam of her lips until her jaw relaxed and he could taste her mouth. Margarita and chocolate. Those were two tastes that shouldn't work together, but in her mouth? Perfect. He broke the kiss, resting his forehead against hers. "I'm going to make love to you, Jolie. It won't be as good or as thorough as I'd wanted for our first time back together—"

"Are we?"

Cord raised his head to look at her. "Are we what?"

"Back together."

His thoughts ran full out on the hamster wheel of his man brain. He knew, instinctively, this was a crossroads. He'd either screw up royally or he'd win this woman back. "That depends on you, I guess."

That intriguing V formed between her brows again, and he kissed it. "I don't want to make assumptions, Jolie. I want us to be friends at the very least. I want to be CJ's dad, not just his sperm donor. I want it to be you and me. Us. We. A couple. But what I want doesn't matter much if you don't want the same thing. What do you want, sunshine? Because from where I'm standin', the ball's in your court."

Aw, hell. Tears spilled from her eyes, turning her long lashes spiky. He'd screwed up. Again. Then she threw her arms around him and rode him down to the bed. "I was right. You are an impossible man. Impossible and perfect and…and…"

Cord kissed her in self-defense. His palm curled around a breast and he smiled as her nipple tightened. He managed to get her bra unhooked and off. Panties slid off easily, and then he had her naked and glorious, and if it was possible, he was even harder.

Jolie helped him out of his trousers and boxers and made him stand there at the side of the bed wearing nothing but his socks. He didn't care. Before she was ready to stop looking, Cord climbed onto the bed and stalked her, socks and all. Still laughing, she scooted up until her back was braced against the pile of pillows shoved against her headboard.

"I'll show you funny," he mock growled at her. Pinning her wrists, he kissed down her side until she squirmed and giggled breathlessly. His Jolie was still ticklish. *His*. Man, he liked the sound of that. He teased her breast, swiping his tongue across the nipple before fastening his lips around it and sucking. She arched into him. She'd always responded so perfectly to his touch. Trailing a hand down her side, he palmed her tummy, and then dipped lower. She gasped and widened her thighs as he cupped her. She was hot and ready for him.

He wasn't drunk this time—unlike that long-ago St. Patrick's Day—and he released her breast to gaze up at her. "Birth control?" He had a condom in his wallet, but hell if he knew where his wallet had ended up.

"Pill. We're good."

"Sunshine, we're much better than good." He settled between her thighs and it felt as if he'd come home. He kissed her fluttering eyelids as he sank deep into her moist center. Stroking in and out of her, he forgot about his injuries. He forgot about anger and hurt and everything but how good it was to have Jolie surrounding him.

He tucked a hand under her hips and urged her to wrap her legs around his waist. She hesitated until the new angle guided him over the one spot guaranteed to roll her eyes back in her head. She gasped and met him stroke for stroke, urging him to push into her faster and deeper.

Cord braced himself on one arm and watched Jolie's face. Her emotions played across it like a movie, and he was positive she felt their connection as acutely as he did. His hips pumped and she rose to meet him, her breath hitching whenever he withdrew.

She whispered something, a one-syllable word that he realized was his name. "Cord." This time she said it louder. "Oh, Cord. Yes…please. Cord…"

And then he was breathing as hard as she was. Lights sparkled in his peripheral vision as his whole body tightened. Jolie's body clenched him, and then he couldn't see anything at all as they exploded together.

Later—much, much later—he managed to get them under the covers, the light turned off and Jolie gathered to his side. He kissed her temple and tangled his hand in her hair as she nestled her head on his shoulder. As she drowsed, memories swamped him. Sex had always been amazing. It was the emotional stuff that twisted them up. Had he ever loved her or was it just sex, just a way to get back at his father?

She murmured something in her sleep and he kissed her forehead. He'd never considered himself to be a tender man, but damn if this woman and the little boy upstairs made him wonder if he could be.

Thirteen

"Mommy? Mommy? Mom!"

Someone groaned in Jolie's ear. Cord. CJ! She bolted up in bed, scrambling to keep the sheet pulled up over her naked chest. The little boy bounced at the foot of the bed with barely contained excitement. She glanced at Cord. He'd pulled a pillow over his head, but continued to groan.

"Stop, CJ."

"Mommy, Daddy's here. Right here." He bounced again and would have fallen on Cord if she hadn't let go of the sheet long enough to grab her son before he landed on his father.

"CJ. Enough. Yes. But be careful. Your dad got hurt."

The boy quieted immediately, eyes wide as he stared at Cord. "You gots a boo-boo?"

"I got a couple of boo-boos, bubba." Cord emerged from beneath the pillow.

"No, Daddy. You didn't gets boo-boos. You gots big owies." CJ crept forward on his hands and knees and very gently poked Cord's face.

"Yeah, you should see the other guys," Cord muttered under his breath.

Jolie bit her lips to keep from giggling. "CJ, you need to go watch TV or something until we get up."

"I'm hungry, Mommy. Can I have pancakes?"

"CJ, go watch TV until your mom and I are ready. Then I'll take you both out for breakfast, and yes, you can have pancakes. But—" Cord held up his index finger "—no pancakes if you come back in here. We'll come out when we're ready."

Her little boy's brow furrowed, and his mouth scrunched up as he considered the implications. Jolie recognized the look and the tactic. She settled back to see how Cord would deal with the subtle blackmail. "Chocolate-chip pancakes?"

"Blueberry."

"With whipped cream?"

"No syrup, then."

"Hmm." CJ crossed his arms and tapped his chin with a finger.

Jolie pulled the sheet up to her nose and coughed away a laugh.

"Can I have little piggies?"

Cord glanced at her for translation. "Link sausage."

"Ah." He appeared to consider the question. "Yes. Blueberry pancakes, whipped cream and little piggies."

"Okay." CJ bounced off the bed. "But hurry, okay? I'm really, really hungry."

Before either of them could respond, the boy raced from the room.

"Shut the door, CJ," Cord called after him. "And no slamming." Seconds later the door slowly swung shut and latched. "Remind me to lock the door next time."

That did it. She lost it, laughing so hard she could barely breathe. When she could talk without giggling, she admitted his performance had impressed her.

"Hey, I was a kid once. I know how boys think. Plus, I'm a better negotiator. I have more practice." He waggled his brows and reached for her. Snagging her wrist, he pulled her back to his side and tucked her in close. "Now, where were we?"

"We were sleeping."

"True, but now that we're awake…" He nudged her chin up so he could capture her mouth with his. He didn't just kiss her. His lips latched on to hers, moving across them, sucking and nibbling. Heat pooled between her legs, making her squirm against him.

Cord brushed his hand down her side, cupping her hip while he deepened the kiss, and then continued down until he'd reached her knee. He hooked his fingers and pulled so that her leg was half sprawled across his groin. She smiled into his kiss. He was very happy to see her this morning.

She broke the kiss. "I need to brush my teeth."

"Too late for that. I've already kissed you, dragon breath. I'm immune now."

She laughed again, but clapped her hand over her mouth. What in the world had gotten into her? Oh, yeah, Cord. That elicited a snorting giggle. Despite the fact they'd been caught in flagrante delicto, Jolie felt freer than she had in… She couldn't remember that far back. Cord was in bed with her, the morning after, hard and wanting her. He hadn't batted an eye when CJ stormed in and woke them. And he wasn't too worried about getting caught making love to her again. She should get up, go lock the door, but she was so…comfortable.

He brushed her hair back over her shoulder and cocked his head. "What?"

Smiling, she stretched to kiss him. "I'm happy. That's all."

"No, sunshine. That's everything. At least to me."

He pulled her over on top of him so she was straddling him. He barely winced as she pushed against his shoulders and straightened. "Raise up, baby," he murmured.

She rocked up on her knees. He fitted his erection at her entrance and she slowly sank down. Breath hissed from his lungs, followed by a quick inhale as she rocked up again. Setting a slow, easy rhythm, Jolie decided she liked being in charge.

"I see what you're thinking up there, pretty girl. Don't get cocky."

She laughed, arching her back and rolling her hips forward. Cord groaned, and she increased the tempo. His large, slightly calloused hands rested on her thighs, and he squeezed gently before moving to grip her hips. The beginnings of her orgasm stirred in her center, and she lost the rhythm for a moment. Cord took over, thrusting up into her, his hands holding her right where he—and she—wanted her.

"Do you know how gorgeous you are?"

Her skin heated and she tucked her chin, once again faltering in her rhythm. Cord cupped her cheek, and then curled his fingers behind her neck to tug her gently down for a kiss. "Don't, sweetheart. You are beautiful. Even more now than when we were kids."

Her protest was swallowed by his kiss. Last night had been hot and heavy and needy. This morning was sweet, forming a connection between them that she'd missed more than she could believe. She didn't want to think about what might have been. She didn't want to remember what had been. She simply wanted here and now, the man she'd never stopped loving filling her.

"Ah, Jolie. What you do to my heart, sunshine."

She stilled, everything slowing—heart, lungs, brain. Noise faded to silence as though her ears had been stuffed with cotton balls. Her vision narrowed to focus on the man lying beneath her and what he'd said, what it might mean. He'd never been one for romantic words. Then he offered that quirky grin and his dimple peeked out. The world rushed back in with a whoosh and she inhaled like a drowning woman coming up for the third time.

"Oh, Cord." Her eyes misted as she lowered herself to kiss him again before tucking her face into his shoulder.

Jolie lay still on top of him. Cord didn't want to move, but he was throbbing inside her. Whatever he'd done, it had been something so right he needed to make notes. And bottle it. So he could do it again. Especially when he made her mad. Then he realized her breaths were coming in little hiccupping sobs. Crap. That couldn't be good. Could it?

He patted her back awkwardly. "Shh, baby. It's okay. I'll fix whatever it is. Don't cry."

"You're impossible," she sniffled.

Well, so much for the moment. He'd screwed up again, obviously. Before he could ask what he'd done wrong, she turned her head and nuzzled down his jawline, careful of his bruises. Her inner muscles squeezed him and he gasped. The reaction wasn't very manly, but the feel of her surrounding him made it hard to breathe.

Rolling his hips, he stroked up gently. She met him with a roll of her own. This he could do. He could finish their lovemaking. Make her feel how much he loved being inside her. With great care, he shifted their positions so she was lying beneath him and he now had more control. Her eyes remained closed but her lips were parted and her tongue and teeth worked her bottom lip. He lowered his head to nip at its plump temptation.

Sweet and slow quickly turned to needy and fast. They came together, and he was so spent his arms shook as he braced above her. Hating to break the connection, he also didn't want to face-plant on her chest or squash her. He leveraged to her side and sank into the mattress.

He lost track of time as he cuddled Jolie to his side. Each time he touched her, each time they made love, it just got better and better. Her presence did wicked things to his body, but it also eased his soul. Cord just managed to swallow the snort that thought prompted. If he spent much more time around this amazing woman, his brothers and cousins would demand he surrender his man card. At this particular moment in time, he would have burned that sucker himself. He didn't want to be anywhere but here.

The shuffle of feet and heavy breathing caught his attention. He glanced toward the door and saw a shadow moving back and forth in the crack under the door. CJ. Who clearly wanted their attention.

"Jolie?"

"Mmm?"

"We need to get up, sunshine. CJ's waiting."

"Mmm."

"Why don't you grab the first shower."

"Mmm?" Her forehead crinkled, and he kissed the V between her brows. He liked it when she made that face and his lips smoothed the wrinkles away.

"Shower. You take longer to get ready so you go first."

"Oh. Right."

Cord didn't mention that he had ulterior motives—such as watching her walk to the bathroom, only to follow a few moments later so he could watch her through the fogged glass shower door. Oh, yeah. He would have to take care of the woody he now sported, but he'd wait for his own shower. If he got in with her now, their son would likely starve to death. His stomach rumbled. Cord would, too, if that noise was any indication.

The shower door slid open and Jolie's face appeared. "Are you watching me?" She sounded outraged, but he knew she wasn't.

"Damn straight I am."

"Pervert."

"Guilty as charged."

Her gaze traveled down his body, stopping at his groin. Something twinkled in her eyes, and Cord couldn't decide if it was lust or humor. "So why don't you join me?" she purred.

He laughed and palmed himself. "Trust me, I'd love to, but then CJ and I both would starve to death."

"Party pooper."

"Somebody has to be the responsible adult."

Jolie giggle-snorted and slapped her hand over her

mouth to diffuse the sound. He widened his stance and crossed his arms over his chest. "I rest my case."

"Oh, okay." She muttered something under her breath that he couldn't decipher before she added, "But you're gonna get yours one of these days."

"I certainly hope so. And I hope that you're the one giving it to me because, honey? I promise I'm gonna be giving it to you."

Before he could react, a sopping sea sponge flew across the room and nailed him right on his pride and joy with a wet splat. Jolie's deadly aim had not diminished with the passage of time. "Careful, woman," he roared.

Stalking toward the shower, full of comical indignation, he plotted his revenge. Jolie cringed in the corner of the stall, which was more than large enough to accommodate two. She'd armed herself with a loofah. Cord plastered a smirk full of male superiority on his face, leaned in and grabbed the handle used to adjust water temperature. He cranked that baby to full cold, slammed the door shut and held it.

"Cord!" Jolie sputtered. "Dang it." She jerked the door handle on her side, and then beat on the glass with the palm of her hand. "Cord, please! It's freezing."

"Of course it is."

"Let me out, Cord. Before I turn into an icicle."

Relenting, he grabbed a towel that had been on the warming rack, opened the door and gathered her into his arms. Wrapping her in the towel, he offered to pat her dry. She impolitely refused.

"Get your shower," she grumped.

Laughing, he leaned in to readjust the temperature. "Sore loser."

"You bet I am. And you'd best remember that." She arched a brow and did her best to scowl at him.

Cord stepped into the shower, but looked at her right before sliding the door closed. "I remember everything about you, Jolie."

Fourteen

Dating Jolie was akin to walking a tightrope. Balancing her needs, CJ's needs and what Cord wanted was a real stretch. Two weeks of swallowing what he wanted in favor of what would win Jolie over. Two weeks of dodging his family, except where business was concerned. The hell of it was, he didn't know if he was making any headway with her. He deserved brownie points for tonight regardless.

They were at the bar of Starr's, waiting for their table. Jolie was doing Jell-O shots, which came under the heading of A Very Bad Idea. The fact that Cord was matching Jolie shot for shot with tequila qualified him as a finalist for Dumbass of the Year.

When he'd picked her up after work, she'd been in an odd mood—quiet and withdrawn. So here they sat. He needed to shovel some food into her. Preferably food with lots of carbs to absorb the alcohol.

"Drinking game."

A puzzled expression furrowed his forehead as Cord attempted to follow her non sequitur. "Drinking game?"

"Yesh. Let's play." She tossed off another shot and shook her finger in his direction. "Things you wish you hadn't done."

This couldn't end well, especially with her already starting to slur her words. "Jolie, you need to eat something."

That got an eyebrow waggle from her before she flagged

down the bartender for another shot. When he returned with a fresh drink, she downed it.

"I'll start." She had to stop and inhale deeply before continuing, "Going to nursing school."

Cord didn't expect that to be the first thing out of her mouth. Before he could ask her why, she banged her glass to get the bartender's attention. "Your turn."

Leaving you. But instead of saying that out loud, he offered a wry smile. "Suggesting we get a drink first instead of going straight in to dinner."

"Oh, pooh. Doesn't count. This ish serioush." She gulped another shot, wiped her lips with the back of her hand and stared at the top of the polished bar. She didn't look up, but Cord watched color drain from her face as she said, "I killed a kid."

And there was the source of her rush to intoxication. "Jolie—"

"Don't *Jolie* me. A little girl died in the ER today. We couldn't save her." Her voice lost the drunken slur in the force of her emotion. "If I hadn't gone to nursing school, I wouldn't have been there. I wouldn't have been responsible."

"You aren't responsible—"

"*I* couldn't save her, Cord." Tears leaked down her cheeks, and he wanted to take her into his arms, protect her from the hurt in her heart.

"C'mon, sunshine. Let's go home." He tossed money on the bar and urged her to stand.

"Not telling you about CJ." Diamond-glazed eyes stared up at him as her voice firmed again. "That's my biggest regret."

"Mine's walking away from you." There. He'd said the words. Truth at last, but she didn't even glance at him.

He kept her tucked under his arm and moving, pausing only briefly to cancel their reservations. Neither of them spoke on the drive to her house, and whenever he glanced over, her eyes remained closed. He got her to the front door and rang the bell rather than dig through her suitcase of a purse to find her keys.

Mrs. Corcoran didn't say a word as he guided Jolie inside, his arm around her waist. When he tried to get her to walk toward her bedroom and she stumbled, he gave up and simply swept her into his arms to carry her. The older woman followed and wordlessly shooed him out after he'd placed Jolie on the bed. The woman was still tsk-tsking when she joined him in the kitchen ten minutes later.

"Good thing CJ is already in bed and asleep. He shouldn't see his mama like that." She glowered at Cord as if Jolie's condition was all his fault.

"She had a rough day. They lost a little girl in the ER."

That news knocked the wind out of Mrs. Corcoran's sails. "Bless her heart. She takes what happens at work so hard. Poor thing."

Her glower returned, and Cord raised his hands in surrender. "She doesn't have to work, ma'am. I'd support her and CJ, or her father would, but she works because she wants to."

"That may well be, but that little lady needs someone to take care of her."

"Absolutely."

Once again, he'd left her speechless—for a few minutes, at least. "So what're you gonna do?"

"My best, Mrs. Corcoran. I'm going to do my best to convince her that the three of us can be a family."

Jolie stared at the rack of Halloween costumes. Where had time gone? How could Halloween be a week away? She and Cord were dating—sort of. And he hadn't mentioned her drunken confession—thankfully, though he'd dumped her and run, rescheduling their dinner for the next night. Still, she would have been mortified if he'd thrown her admission in her face. Instead, he pushed for more in their relationship.

In general, though, she didn't allow Cord to spend the night; they used his place as a stopover for sex before he took her home. With the arrival of cooler weather, he grumbled about getting out of a warm bed. She knew he wanted more from her. He wanted a commitment—one she wasn't ready to give. She hadn't forgiven him for breaking up with her, and wasn't sure she ever wanted to.

Her focus had to be CJ, what was good for her son. She had such mixed feelings about Cord—and his family. CJ was no longer the shy little boy clinging to her hand when she dropped him off at preschool. As much as she hated to admit it, Cord's influence had something to do with that. Okay, he had a lot to do with it.

They did *guy* things together—Cord and CJ. They'd gone fishing. He'd taught CJ to ride, and her son was turning into a cowboy fanatic. He refused to wear anything but Western boots—just like his dad's. Jeans were de rigueur. They both had black felt Stetsons, creased and shaped identically. Cord had a picture of them dressed up—same hats, shirts, belt buckles, jeans and boots. They were two peas in a pod, and he displayed the framed photo on his desk for everyone to see. He was so dang proud of being a dad.

Cord got to be the good guy, the parent who gave treats and fun times. She was the parent stuck with the responsibility. She administered time-outs and bedtimes, and said no. Whenever CJ returned from one of their outings, it was "Daddy this" and "Daddy that" and "Daddy and me." Her son had no room in his thoughts for her. She was losing him as Cord seduced CJ away with promises and presents.

She didn't want Cord in her life. Did she? Oh, the sex between them was as hot as it had always been. But sex wasn't enough. She'd thought they had something back in college. Something real and permanent. Boy howdy, had she been wrong about that. And her easy seduction of him on that fateful St. Patrick's Day was proof. The man's brains all resided below his fancy Western belt buckle. And no matter how good he looked in those butt-hugging jeans he favored, no matter how sweet he was to her son, Cord was still Cord *Barron*. The Barrons were…Barrons. Egotistical. Overbearing. Thinking they were entitled to anything they wanted. No matter how much Cord professed to have changed, had he? And what about Cyrus Barron? He was bound to find out about CJ sooner than later. What then? What would Cord do? But more important, how could she let CJ be around the hateful old man who was his grandfather simply because they shared DNA?

Jolie couldn't figure out why—or when—her thoughts had turned so negative where Cord was concerned. Being honest, she could admit that since he'd dumped her at home, left to Mrs. Corcoran's tender mercies after getting drunk, she tended to snarl whenever thoughts of him cropped up. She didn't discuss her feelings with him. He said he knew her. He should know what was bothering her. And besides, it was just like a man to cut and run. Especially this one. He had the history for it. Things got tough? Cord Barron disappeared. Except he hadn't yet. He wanted to officially acknowledge CJ, make things legal. She panicked at the idea. She didn't want to hand over that kind of control to him.

Noise filtered back into her consciousness, and she shook away the negative thoughts. Halloween was coming and CJ needed a costume. Jolie flicked through the nearly empty rack and pulled out an Iron Man suit and held it up. CJ shook his head, arms folded stubbornly across his chest. What happened to September? There was no way Halloween should be right around the corner. Oh, wait… Cord. He'd filled her time—even when he gave her time off from CJ. In fact, Cord had volunteered to escort CJ and some of his friends when they went trick-or-treating, but she wanted to go, too. She checked the size on the Spider-Man costume.

"No, Mommy. I don't wanna be a superhero."

"Fine. Then what do you want to be?"

"I told you. I wanna be a cowboy. Like Daddy." He shoved his hands in his pockets and slid her a sly glance from the corner of his eyes.

She didn't like that look at all. "What?"

"Nothin'."

"CJ?" She used her this-is-your-only-warning voice when she said his name.

"If I go as a cowboy, Daddy might bring a horse."

Jolie did not want to ask. She inhaled, but then screwed her eyes shut and exhaled, knowing she'd regret it. She had to ask anyway. "A real horse?"

"Uh-huh." CJ's eyes crinkled from his ear-to-ear grin. "How cool is that, Mommy? I told all my friends. We're all gonna be cowboys!"

Oh, boy. She didn't know whether to kill Cord or leave him to the mercy of his son's disappointment. Making out-landish promises always had consequences, and the sooner Cord figured that out, the better. He'd worked really hard at spending time with CJ and managing to act like a father—at least the times he wasn't trying to win her over. If she didn't stay on top of things, Cord would spoil their son rotten without a second thought. He needed to learn not to do that because she wasn't going to clean up his messes whenever he brought CJ home. She would *not* be painted as the bad guy because she made and enforced the rules. As much as she didn't want to, she had to sit down with Cord and spell out the ground rules.

If she was honest with herself, she needed to spell out the rules to herself, as well. She didn't mean to fall into his easy trap. He was always there, wanting to see CJ…to see *her*. It was easy to be with him as if time hadn't passed, as if he hadn't broken her heart, as if she hadn't broken his. How did one get over that? She didn't think there was enough superglue in the whole world to mend her heart.

Despite Cord's sweetness and apparent concern—now. She swallowed her frustration. He'd always been sweet, but she couldn't trust him to stay.

Her cell phone buzzed with the chorus from Kelly Clarkson's "Since U Been Gone." *Speak of the devil.* She swiped her finger across the face of the phone, her lip curling far enough to wrinkle her nose as she answered, "What do you want?"

Warm laughter filled her ear before Cord's voice followed. "I think you miss me, sunshine."

"Don't flatter yourself. What the heck did you promise CJ about Halloween?"

Silence. She couldn't even hear him breathe. He finally replied, his tone cautious. "Halloween?"

"You're coming to take him trick-or-treating, yes?"

"Yes." Cord drew out the word, making it sound like two syllables.

"He wants to be a cowboy."

"And?" Again, two syllables.

"Are you bringing him a horse?" Silence again. She was ready to light into him when she heard a deep inhalation.

"Not exactly?"

"Don't answer a question with a question, Cord. What *did* you say?"

"Ah…didn't you just answer a—"

"Shut up, Cord." Her exasperation leaked out. Why did she have to be the only adult? "Just explain, okay?"

"Okay. I told CJ that we could have a Halloween party at the ranch. We'd do a hayride and the kids could ride horses in the corral."

"Without asking me?" She made sure her voice sounded frigid. How dare he do this! The man kept insinuating himself into her son's life. Despite all his sweet words and *good* intentions, she wondered at his real motivations. Deep down, she realized, she didn't entirely trust Cord.

"Uh…not exactly? I told him that we'd talk to you. And

that if there wasn't enough time to do it for Halloween, then we'd do it for his birthday."

A band tightened around Jolie's chest, cutting off any air she might be able to suck into her lungs. His birthday? Cord was making plans for CJ's birthday and hadn't bothered to ask her? "You're presuming a helluva lot."

"Bad Mommy. That's a dollar in the swear jar."

She'd forgotten CJ was standing there listening to her. "I can't talk now. We'll discuss this later."

"By which you mean that you'll dictate terms to me and expect me to fall in line. That's not going to work anymore, Jolie. I've been patient, but now I want things official. I want to be CJ's father legally. I'll pick you up for dinner tonight. We'll go somewhere quiet where we can talk this through."

Dead air. He'd hung up on her. Before she could hang up on him. She grabbed CJ's hand without a word and turned toward the exit.

"I don't wanna go. Mommy." He braced his feet and pulled back against her grip.

People stared, some stopping and turning to watch. Jolie closed her eyes and breathed deeply to center herself. When had she become such a raging shrew? Easy answer—the moment Cord had walked back into her life. Even if he'd been strapped to a gurney and almost dead at the time. She knelt down and curled her fingers over CJ's shoulders. "Look, Mommy is very angry at your father right now. I shouldn't take it out on you, but do me a favor, okay? Just c'mon. No fighting. No whining."

His bottom lip quivered and Jolie wanted to bang her head against the nearest wall. Instead, she rose and held out her hand. CJ took it and she led him from the store. She had to get a grip on herself and control of the situation with Cord. She'd allowed him far too much leeway in her son's life. And now he wanted it legal? He'd take complete control because that was what Barrons did. CJ was *her* son.

Except…CJ was Cord's, too. Guilt raised its head like some stupid Whac-a-mole. No matter how many times she clobbered the feeling with a sledgehammer, it just reappeared to suck out all her resolve.

Emotion roiled inside her—a flash flood hitting a dam with a pounding rush. The water level kept rising, and one of two things was going to happen. Her emotions would spill over the top and slowly relieve some of the pressure or she'd drown in them. She couldn't afford for either event to happen. She could not lose control. Not of CJ, which she would if Cord continued to press his parental rights. Not of her heart if the man continued to assault her with his easy smiles and sexy ways. Her life teetered on the edge of a precipice. Part of her wanted to snort at the analogy but she couldn't. That was the way she felt.

She had to make a stand. Sooner, not later.

Fifteen

As soon as she entered the restaurant, Jolie knew this was a stupid move on her part. She'd refused to let Cord pick her up, insisting she'd drive herself and meet him there. The stupid part was letting him pick the restaurant—his compromise to her unyielding "no" and for stalling this meeting until after Halloween. He'd shown up to take her to dinner the night before Halloween but she'd dodged a confrontation by taking an extra shift at work.

Then Cord had arrived Halloween evening to take the kids trick-or-treating, and according to Mrs. Corcoran, he'd come with a compromise—a handmade stick horse for CJ to "ride." She'd volunteered for extra duty at the ER with Operation X-ray as an excuse to avoid Cord. As community outreach, Trauma One offered to X-ray Halloween candy for hidden dangers. She had plausible deniability, since that volunteer time was important. She wasn't afraid to face him. Not at all.

The host led her on a winding trail through tables filled with couples. This was so not a family restaurant. The thought of CJ eating here sent cold chills through her. This was a date place—for men out to impress their ladies, for parents to get away from the kids to remember they could still be in love. Low lights, soft music, a place steeped in romance.

Pristine white cloths draped the tables. Crystal and silver gleamed in flickering candlelight. Delicate but aromatic flowers flowed from sparkling vases on each table. Cord was already there, sitting at a table in a secluded corner. He stood as soon as he saw her. He appeared stoic. Dang, but the man had some kind of poker face. She'd always hated that about him—all the Barron brothers, in fact. Dealing with them had taught her, though. She continued to work on her own demeanor.

Something flickered in his eyes as she neared. She did her best to ignore it, but little frissons of awareness skittered across her skin. Even wary, she wanted him. She always had. Candlelight danced across his face. It pasted shadows where none should be. And it added light to places that should have been dark.

Cord nodded to the host and the man veered away, leaving her on her own to face him. He gracefully held her chair, scooting it beneath her thighs as she sat. He bent while doing so and brushed his cheek across her hair.

"You're beautiful."

The words whispered across her consciousness, leaving goose bumps on her psyche. *No. No, no, no, no.* She stiffened her spine and raised her chin. She would not succumb to Mr. Cowboy Sexy, even if he did look good enough for dessert. As he settled back into his chair, she studied him. She could see the candle flame in the depths of his burned-honey eyes. He wore his hair shorter now, a result of part of it being shaved in the hospital, but it was growing out. A dark comma accented his forehead while shadows defined the planes of his face.

No one would doubt Cord and his brothers were related. Somehow, though, he'd ended up with slightly softer features. He was still rugged, with the dark black hair and golden-brown eyes of his siblings. They were all handsome as sin and just as irresistible to the female population. Cord was more relaxed than the others, except maybe Chase. Chase was a horse of a totally different color, living only for wine, women and song. She pitied any woman insane enough to get involved with him. Heck, she was insane to be sitting here with Cord, and he was the nice brother. What did that tell the world about the Barrons?

"A penny for your thoughts."

His husky voice vibrated over her skin and she tensed up. She needed to be on her guard, not sitting here daydreaming about how sexy this man was. He was not above using that—or any other advantage he might gain—against her. They had things to settle here and now. She could not lose sight of that.

"I'm not sure you want to know."

"That's where you'd be wrong, Jolie. I want to know everything about you."

"According to you, you already do."

The corner of his mouth quirked in that devil-may-care grin that once melted her heart. Over and over and over again. Not anymore. She arched a brow in response and he laughed. Reaching across the table, his big hand enveloped hers. She fought the urge to turn hers palm up and twine her fingers with his. Not even the waiter's appearance provided enough of a diversion for her to pull away.

Arrogant as always, Cord ordered for both of them. The fact that he picked the entrée she would have chosen only served to make her angrier, and reinforce the idea he did know her far better than he should.

His expression smoothed out into that blank poker face the Barrons were infamous for. "You're the one who said you wanted to talk to me back before Halloween—and you've avoided me for over a week now. I want to talk about Thanksgiving. Every time I bring up the subject, you shut me down."

Or she diverted him. He'd been talking about Thanksgiving for almost a month. Luckily, the man was easy. A few kisses and caresses and they were off to bed for some fantastic sex. Cord couldn't think beyond the sexy bits. Jolie knew getting intimate was a bad idea but she couldn't seem to help herself. He was still the only man who made her toes curl with a kiss. But he wanted more than sex. He'd been clear about that from the moment he'd discovered CJ was his. He'd wanted joint custody but she didn't. CJ was hers and had been for his whole life. The idea of giving up any control at all terrified her.

Cord squeezed her hand, pulling her attention from the serious intent in his eyes to the way he held her hand— with strength and gentleness. Too bad he hadn't handled her heart the same way.

"This is not the time or the place, Cord."

"Wrong. This *is* the time and place because we're both here."

"I can get up and leave anytime I want."

"Yes. You can." He released her hand, leaned back in his chair and stared at her. Temper glinted in his eyes now. "Are you going to run forever?"

Her nostrils flared and her eyes narrowed. "Wow. You just had to go there, didn't you?" She leaned forward, forearms braced on the table. "I'm not the one who ran."

Cord smirked. It was that or reach across the table and shake her until her teeth rattled. He'd never laid a hand on a woman in anger and he wasn't about to start now. "Pot, kettle, sweetheart." He watched her throat work as she swallowed. Hard. He'd hit the mark with that one. "We both ran. I've admitted I was stupid. You, on the other hand—"

"What about me?" She interrupted him, her green eyes flashing despite the low lights in the restaurant. Oh, yeah. She was pissed now.

"You hid my son from me." The thought still rankled. He'd tried in the past few months to understand her motivations, to forgive her. Getting to know CJ and spending time with Jolie had helped a long way toward that. Until now. Cord didn't understand why she was being so stubborn— why she was shoving him away and blocking his right to acknowledge his son.

"So what? You didn't deserve him."

She flung the words like a shotgun blast, and they blew a hole in his heart. "You didn't exactly give me a chance, did you?" He choked back his hurt and anger, keeping his voice soft, with no inflection. What the hell had gotten into her? "He *is* my son, Jolie. I have the results from the paternity test."

Her mouth dropped open as her eyes rounded in shock. "You went behind my back? You ran a test on him without my permission?"

"I knew from the moment I saw him he was mine. The DNA test is for the lawyers. To cover the legal bases."

"Lawyers?" She spit the word out like a bitter pill—or maybe he was the only one who felt that way. He didn't want to go to court, but Jolie was very quickly leaving him little choice in the matter. Cyrus, as soon as he had found out, made threats to do things his way. Chance would keep things on an even keel—and civil. Cyrus wouldn't.

The sommelier arrived and served their wine with no fanfare. He'd obviously picked up on their mood. Their waiter slid in right behind him, efficiently depositing their salads and moving away without a word.

Cord sipped his wine, watching her over the rim of the crystal flute. She sat so rigid her muscles were almost spasming. Her hands were hidden in her lap, but he'd lay odds they were clasped tightly together. He wanted to gather her into his arms, kissing her until she let go, until she admitted he was right. He wanted her, dammit. And CJ. They could be a family. He was positive of it. He just needed Jolie to understand. And to agree. He reached into his jacket pocket and fingered the velvet box hidden there. He'd hoped to convince her they could be a family, and he'd taken to carrying the ring as a good luck charm. And if he were honest, he'd admit he was considering proposing tonight, if things went his way.

All he had to do was chip away at her anger. He'd already breached her defenses where making love was concerned. She desired him as much as he wanted her. He had her body. Now he wanted her heart, and he'd solemnly promised himself he'd take far better care of that treasure than he had the first time. Once Jolie agreed to marriage, they were a done deal—one Cyrus had no control over.

He swallowed his anger with the next sip of wine and allowed a fleeting smile to show as she attacked her salad, stabbing innocent greens with a fork. Cord was positive she was picturing that fork buried over and over in his chest. Setting his wine aside, he picked up his fork and ate calmly, a counterpoint to her frenzy she wouldn't appreciate. That was all part of his plan. He had to keep her off balance to get what he wanted. Her. CJ. A life and family together.

"Can we talk about Thanksgiving, Jolie? Why don't you and CJ come out to the ranch? Cassie and Miz Beth are pulling out all the stops so we can have a real family get-together. If you're worried about my old man, don't be. As soon as Cassie started organizing a family dinner, he made plans to fly to Vegas. He'll be at the Crown Casino for the long weekend."

He offered what he hoped was a disarming grin. "Heck, Clay is coming into town for it. He's bringing his speechwriter to work on campaign stuff, but he'll be there. Cassie even managed to lure Chase back to town, assuming he doesn't back out at the last minute." He watched her but couldn't decide her mood.

Jolie paused in her chewing to offer him another glare before returning her gaze to her plate. He leaned over the table and lowered his voice to a conspiratorial undertone. "Don't tell anyone, but I think Cyrus is actually afraid of Cassie." He bit back laughter when she glanced up, startled. He winked and continued, "I know the rest of us are. As for Cyrus, Cash thinks he has a showgirl on speed dial, and with Chase back here for Thanksgiving, the old man will have free rein."

A busboy appeared and whisked their used plates and utensils away while refilling water glasses. Moments later, the waiter arrived and served their entrées. The man waited stoically while he and Jolie sampled a taste and nodded their satisfaction. Cord bit back a sigh. He would have taken her to Cattlemen's for dinner, but this was her sort of restaurant, and honestly, he wanted to impress her. Just because he preferred jeans and boots didn't mean he couldn't dress up. Like all the Barrons, he could move in what he called the silk-panty social circles. The Barrons commanded incredible wealth. J. Rand Davis did, too. Hell, the man had written a check for half a million dollars to Cord's sister-in-law, drawn on his personal account. Cord was still chapped that J. Rand had warned him away from Jolie that day.

He didn't like where his thoughts were headed, so he reined them in and concentrated on the problem at hand. Jolie continued to eat, ignoring him again. He was tired of playing that game. "What happened to you?"

Her head snapped up and she glared at him. Her "laser death stare" was probably lethal to anyone but him. He thought the look was adorable, but he hid his smile.

"What happened to me? I have no idea what you're talking about."

"I think you do." He leaned forward again and this time dropped his voice to a husky whisper. "What happened to the cowgirl who used to ride bareback and take her horse swimming in the lake? Where's the girl who sat in the bleachers cheering me on at the rodeo?"

Her face paled, but she held his gaze. "You, Cord. That's what happened to me. You walked in, told me you were done and walked out. That girl no longer exists."

Jolie's words sliced his heart as she'd meant them to. He bit back the retort forming on his tongue, breathing through the emotional pain as he continued to watch her. As he knew she would, she dropped her gaze. Neither of them truly had the high moral ground in this thing between them. "That's too bad. She was special."

He reached for the wine bottle and refilled their glasses. Jolie gulped hers, looking for liquid courage. He sipped again, needing to keep his wits about him. He'd worked too hard to nurture the tiny sprouts of feelings she'd developed for him to ruin it by snapping back at her. He'd already done damage tonight with his sharp retorts, which became obvious when he watched her eyes skitter back and forth as she looked anywhere but him. He softened his voice to add, "She still is."

"What are you doing, Cord?"

"Trying to talk to you. About CJ. About us."

"I don't want to talk."

He took another sip of wine, watching her, assessing her mood. "Why didn't you tell me?"

"We've been over this."

"Yes. And you still haven't been honest with me."

Jolie closed her eyes and her shoulders drooped. Cord almost felt sorry for her. He definitely wanted to take her in his arms, hold and kiss her, to tell her how he felt, that everything would be all right, over and over again until she believed him. Instead, he waited—outwardly calm but coiled like a tight spring on the inside.

"It was a one-night stand, Cord. That's all. Payback. I didn't have feelings for you anymore."

"Liar." He smiled when he said the word.

"I didn't," she protested. "And then, bam. Two months later, I find out I'm pregnant. I know how you think. How all of you think. I'm not stupid."

"I never thought you were." His forehead furrowed in consternation. "But I'm confused. What are you talking about?"

"You. Your brothers. How many paternity suits have been brought against you?"

He blinked in surprise. "Me? None. Clay's cleaner than a

bottle of bleach. Chance was too careful. Same with Cash." His lips curled into a wry smirk. "Chase, however, has probably made the headlines more than he should. But, sunshine, that has nothing to do with us. With you and me."

"Don't *sunshine* me." Jolie huffed out a breath that ruffled her bangs. "Still."

"Still what?"

"Just…still. You didn't love me. I didn't want to trap you into a relationship that you'd end up hating me for. Besides, you wouldn't have listened."

His smile disappeared, and he leaned close enough to cup her cheek in his palm. "Do you believe that? That I didn't love you?" Had he never told her? He couldn't, for his life, remember if he had or not. Had she ever said the words to him? To his embarrassment, he couldn't remember that, either. He'd just assumed she knew how he felt. "I did. I do." He shoved his other hand back into his pocket, closing his fingers around the box, but he could already feel the moment slipping away. Until he was fairly certain she'd say yes, Cord was not going to ask her to marry him.

"You're just saying that."

"No, sunshine, I'm not. I do love you. I love CJ, too. I want the world to know he's my son—that we made something special together."

She tilted her head away from his hand, so he dropped it to the table and leaned back. "You need to stay away, Cord."

"That's not going to happen. CJ is mine. No matter what I have to do, I'm going to make sure of that."

"What do you mean?"

"Exactly what I've been saying all along. I want to be a part of CJ's life. And yours. I want to take care of you both."

"We don't need you to take care of us." Her eyes narrowed in speculation and worry. "Make sure of what? What have you done?" Her face flushed and her hands once again twisted in her lap.

Jolie believed she was always in control of her emotions.

Cord knew better. He'd swallowed her screams as she came apart in his arms when they'd made love. He'd absorbed her tears and anger. He'd made her laugh and had laughed with her. She was his everything, no matter what she said.

"Nothing." His gaze never left her face. "Yet. Chance drafted some paperwork. CJ is my son. I want to petition the court to issue an amended birth certificate." He covered her hands with his and she tensed. "You know I want to be his father legally, Jolie. It's for his protection."

She jerked away and scooted her chair back. He tunneled his fingers through his hair. "The accident made me think, sunshine. About the future. About my life. I didn't know CJ even existed, but I do now. I could have died. I want to make sure our son is provided for."

Jolie hissed like a cat dunked in a bucket of cold water. "I have more than enough assets to take care of CJ. And Dad set up a trust when he was born."

"He's still my son, Jolie. I want us to be a family."

"No." She looked around in a panic. "I'm not ready for this, Cord."

Cord concentrated on remaining calm. "Please don't fight me, Jolie. I don't want to go to court. For CJ's sake."

"If you really cared about CJ, you'd drop this. You can hang around with him. That's fine. But you aren't his father. No matter how many papers you file. You never will be."

"Never? That's not a threat you want to make."

Sixteen

Cord watched Cassie and Miz Beth maneuver around each other in the kitchen. Big John sprawled on one of the oversize stools pulled up to the breakfast bar, begging for tastes with big puppy-dog eyes. The women laughed and teased him as they sailed by, intent on chores only they could accomplish. Cash and Chase played pool in the game room, volleying good-natured, if loud, bets with each stroke of the pool cue. Chance and CJ were flipping through TV channels waiting for the football games to start.

The only Barron brother missing was Clay. He was in the house, but holed up in the study with his speechwriter, Georgie. Politics were afoot and Cord suspected his US Senator brother was looking into a run at the presidency. This was a working vacation for Clay. Georgie had no family as far as Cord knew, so she'd been welcomed into the impromptu family group for Thanksgiving.

He had only one regret. Jolie had refused to come. The fight they'd had three weeks ago still stank up the atmosphere. He hadn't meant to push things, but he was tired of waiting. He wanted her to agree that he had a legal—and emotional—right to CJ. And her. He wanted to marry her, wanted them to be a family. He glanced around again. She'd fit right in with Miz Beth and Cassie. His brothers would come to love her, too.

He'd cajoled, Jolie had haggled and finally they had compromised. He'd proved Cyrus would not make an appearance and she'd reluctantly relented, allowing CJ to come for Thanksgiving. He'd asked her to come again when he'd picked up CJ that morning. She'd refused, tight-lipped and still angry, muttering about his father's shortcomings. She was right. Cyrus wasn't prone to family occasions. He'd left that up to the mothers who'd provided his sons. After Helen, the second Mrs. Barron's death, each wife du jour got younger and younger, and they usually wanted to travel to exotic places rather than deal with a pack of rowdy boys. Miz Beth and Big John had organized the holidays. Birthday parties. Thanksgiving with all the trimmings. Christmas. They'd provided chocolate bunnies and Easter egg hunts, Fourth of July watermelons and Halloween trick-or-treating.

Feeling melancholy, Cord wandered into the great room and sank into one of the massive leather chairs. Sprawling his legs out, he pasted a smile on his face as CJ started jabbering about football teams and who he wanted to win. Chance caught Cord's eye above the boy's head and winked. He grinned at his brother, surprised by the feelings of contentment stealing over him. They hadn't gathered as a family since Chance's wedding. They'd paused in their busy lives to celebrate, and then scattered almost as soon as the reception ended. Cord's near-death experience didn't count because his brothers had visited in shifts. Today was different—laid-back, Clay's work notwithstanding.

The ranch house had evolved through the years, and it now rivaled the house they'd occupied in Nichols Hills when it came to size and amenities. The mansion had never felt like home. This place did. Pictures of all of them as kids lined the rough-hewn fireplace mantel. Colorful Southwest-patterned rugs and blankets added cheer to the great room. The homey scents of roasting turkey, pumpkin pie and baking rolls perfumed the air. Cord wanted this feeling. Wanted this sense of family with his heart and soul. All he needed to do was win Jolie back.

Before he could focus on what he should do to ensure his success, Cassie called them to the table. CJ happily dashed through the house to get "Uncle Clay and the pretty lady." When they were seated, more feelings of family swamped Cord. The massive oak table had come down through the family. Scarred, sanded and refinished countless times through the generations, it was one of the few stable things in their lives. Miz Beth sat at the end nearest the kitchen. Georgie, Clay's assistant, sat on Miz Beth's right, Clay beside her, then Cord and CJ. Big John sat at the other end. On his right down the opposite side sat Cassie, Chance, Chase and Cash. There was room for even more chairs.

Big John said grace, and then food was passed around the table, the Barron brothers fighting over drumsticks, white meat, olives and rolls. CJ had pitted black olives stuck on all the fingers of his left hand and was eating them one by one. No one told him that was rude. This was Thanksgiving.

Dinner ended with pumpkin, pecan, rhubarb, apple and chocolate meringue pies, and CJ winning the wishbone break with Cash—a family tradition for the two youngest Barron males. CJ chortled and bounced on his toes beside the table.

"I win. I win, Uncle Cash. What do I win?"

Rolling his eyes, Cash pushed back from the table and stood. "Ask your father." He turned on his heel and strode away, angry for a reason Cord couldn't fathom. CJ's exuberance captured his attention.

"Daddy, Daddy, what do I win?"

"You get a wish, CJ. And since you won, your wish is supposed to come true."

Cassie slipped her hand into Chance's, smiling at the little boy as she asked, "What do you wish for, CJ?"

A look that Cord almost thought sly slid across his son's face before he spoke. "I want a dog. An' a horse. And Mommy and Daddy."

Cord grabbed CJ and hugged him tightly. "Good wish, bubba."

An hour later, dishes were done and the football game was playing on the massive plasma-screen television. CJ was all but asleep on the floor in front of the TV. Cassie and Georgie visited quietly in a small sitting area off the great room. Big John snored in his chair and Miz Beth had disappeared with a picnic basket. Cord suspected she'd headed to Kaden's house. He'd been surprised the foreman wasn't present. Miz Beth would only say that he'd been invited, but had declined. His brothers had disappeared, but Cord didn't care.

Full and happy, he sprawled in the chair, legs propped on the matching ottoman. His eyes drifted shut as the commentators droned on the TV. Family. His might be dysfunctional, but he truly believed they were finally getting their lives in order and their loyalties on track. Then his phone dinged. A text message.

Cord sat up and rubbed his eyes. The women were visiting in the kitchen while Big John and CJ napped through the football game on TV. He checked the message.

COME TO OLD MANS CONF RM 4 MEETING

Cash had sent it. Cord heaved out of the chair and headed toward the hallway that led deeper into the private areas of the house. The room next to the study had been set up as a conference room. Chance sat on the near side of the table. Looking more like twins than ever, Chase and Cash sat opposite him. Clay sat at one end, and the old man himself occupied the chair at the head. What the hell was Cyrus doing back? Cord's first thought centered on Jolie, and he was glad she hadn't come. His second took a moment to catch up. This wasn't a meeting. This was a Barron family intervention.

When had his father arrived? And why hadn't Chance

warned him? Too late now. He stared at each of his brothers. Chase and Clay had the good graces not to meet his gaze. Cash smirked and arched a brow. Chance offered a slight nod—the only sign of solidarity he'd get in this group. Now knowing how Chance had felt last spring when they'd all ganged up on him over Cassie, Cord braced his shoulder against the doorjamb.

"Took you long enough." His father's glare went nuclear when Cord simply lifted a shoulder in acknowledgment. "Sit down." Cyrus gritted out the order.

"Thanks, but I'm comfortable right here." Oh, yeah. He had the height advantage standing up and wasn't about to relinquish it.

Cyrus grimaced and turned his baleful stare on Clay, who had to swivel uncomfortably around in his chair to speak directly to Cord. The glance was his older brother's cue to deliver the coup de grâce. Cord waited, more curious than worried.

Clay cleared his throat, unusual for the brother raised to be first and foremost in the public eye. "Cord, please come in and sit down."

"I can't stay long, Clay. I have to get CJ home. Spit out whatever words the old man is putting in your mouth so we can all get back to our lives."

Cash snorted and leaned back in his chair, the picture of negligent disdain. "I'll spit it out. You need to sign the papers Chance drew up to get your son away from that bi—"

No one had a chance to intercept him as Cord came over the top of the conference table, sliding across the polished surface to land on his feet in front of Cash's chair. He knocked Cash backward and twisted his fist in his brother's pristine shirtfront. "You watch your mouth, little brother. Jolie is the mother of my child. You will speak of her with respect."

The room had gone dead silent. Cash had a couple of inches and about twenty pounds on him, and Cord still wasn't back to 100 percent from the accident, but he was so filled with righteous anger that he was positive he could take the other man. He might be mad at Jolie, but no one in his family had the right to say anything about her.

Cash's smirk widened, but he lowered his eyes in a brief display of submission. Cord loosened his grip, straightened and with a deliberate stride, returned to the doorway. "That goes for the rest of you. CJ is *my* son. I'm dealing with this situation." At least he hoped he could without things escalating further. Due to Jolie's continued stubbornness on the matter, he wasn't too sure.

His gaze zeroed in on his father. "I'm not a stupid frat boy anymore, old man. You keep that in mind. What I do with Jolie and *our* son is none of your business." He pinned each of his brothers with the same glare. "That goes for the rest of you, as well. We clear?"

Nobody moved. Chase continued to stare at his hands lying clasped in his lap. Cash glared back. Clay briefly met his gaze before looking away. Chance's eyes twinkled, though his expression gave nothing away. This was all the satisfaction Cord would get from his brothers, but he hammered the point home with his father. "I mean it, Cyrus. I know you. I know what you did to Chance and Cassie. I'm warning you here and now. Don't mess with Jolie and CJ. Don't mess with me."

His old man slowly clapped his hands in derisive applause. "You always were a disappointment, boy. I've given you time and enough rope to tie up this deal, but you've always been weak. That boy is a Barron. He belongs with his family. Get it done. Or else." He glanced at Clay. "My study, now." Pivoting, Cyrus headed to the connecting door. Clay exhaled a heavy breath, rose and followed their father. The door closed behind him, the sharp sound like a period ending the conversation.

Cord turned to duck out the door, ignoring the twins, but he offered Chance a brief tuck of his chin in acknowledgment of Chance's support. He needed to grab CJ and get the hell away. Sometimes it really sucked to be a Barron. He didn't believe for a New York minute that his father would back down. Cyrus wanted control—of his companies, his sons and now his grandson, and the old man wasn't squeamish when it came to playing dirty.

Halfway along the hall, a closed door caught his attention. The back stairs to the playroom. The hairs on his neck prickled. He hadn't been up there since...he couldn't remember when. He wanted to go up, look around, but hesitated. Surely Clay would keep their father occupied for a while. He'd have time to satisfy his curiosity before taking CJ back to Jolie. He opened the door and slipped through. The bare-wood stairs were dusty. Considering Miz Beth's almost obsessive need to clean, the neglect surprised him. The steps stopped at a wide landing with a door. A right turn led to a long hallway that curved back toward the bedrooms.

The thick wooden door looked just as he remembered it—odd colors of flaking paint, wrought iron hinges and door handle, grooves embedded in the wood. He traced his fingers over the scratches and spelled out each of their names, carved meticulously with a pocket knife. He still had a scar on his hand from the exercise. He pressed the handle and pushed. The door swung open on rusty hinges. He stepped inside and flicked the light switch. Nothing happened. Unerringly, he crossed the floor to the nearest window.

Cord flicked the blinds and watched dust motes dance in the late-afternoon sunlight. He hadn't stepped inside this room in years. Part nursery, part playroom, it contained the detritus of five boys growing up. Clay's bookcase full of biographies and histories. Chance's hard-plastic palomino spring horse, its metal frame rusty. Mud-stained equipment bags full of leather gloves and baseball bats belonging to Cash and Chase. A deep set of shelves under one of the room's windows that held games and a whole motor pool of toy trucks and cars. He smiled and hoped CJ liked trucks as much as he had. He'd bet money half of his collection was still buried out in the yard somewhere.

Picking through boxes, he relived memories from childhood. Not all of them were good, which added a layer of melancholy to his search. He glanced around and realized there was something up here he wanted to look at. He found what he'd been searching for over in the corner. The Barron family cradle, the wood carved and shaped by the hands of his great-great-grandfather. Five generations of Barron babies had slept in that cradle. He rubbed dust off with his hand, fingering the spindles turned on a hand lathe. Five generations. But not the sixth. Not his son.

Jolie had robbed him of that by stealing his son away, by running from him without a word. He'd missed almost five years of his son's life. And her pregnancy. A profound sadness settled on his shoulders. Every time he tried to talk to her about it, she threw up walls.

You wouldn't have listened.

She'd flung the words at him as if they shielded her from responsibility. He damn well was listening now, wasn't he? *She* was the one turning deaf ears to him. Fine. He was a Barron and so was CJ. Cordell Joseph Barron, even if the damn birth certificate listed Davis as his last name.

Tunneling his fingers through his hair, he worked to calm down as he tried to figure out why they continued to fight over this. He still had every intention of asking her to marry him. Even now, the velvet box resided in the pocket of his leather jacket currently hanging downstairs. He wanted official acknowledgment that CJ was his son. He thought he'd made a simple request. *CJ is my son. I want to petition the court to issue an amended birth certificate.* The kid had his own room at the ranch as well as one at Cord's condo in Oklahoma City. Jolie admitted CJ was his. What was the big deal? But she'd freaked out. Big-time. What was she afraid of?

Cord toyed with his cell phone. He wanted to talk to Jolie. No, he *needed* to talk to her. He'd been patient. He'd courted her, given her space and done everything he knew how to reassure her. Christmas was just around the corner. He wanted his family together for the holidays. Jolie and CJ were his family. The best Christmas present in the world would be his name on CJ's birth certificate and his engagement ring on Jolie's left hand. What was wrong with that?

Evidently everything, judging by Jolie's reaction. He hadn't even gotten to the proposal yet. She didn't trust him. She'd tossed that little gem into his lap, too. Well, trust was a two-way street, and he realized he didn't quite trust her, either. She'd kept their son a secret from him. Anger swelled, deep and raging as bile rose in his throat. He swallowed it down.

"Getting mad isn't the answer," he muttered. He'd get even. That was what Barrons did, right? He had the results from the paternity test. CJ was his. Chance had the papers ready to file. The devil on his shoulder tempted him to give Chance the go-ahead to file suit. Which would be the worst thing he could do. Inhaling the dust and mustiness in the air, he huffed out a breath. He needed to forgive and forget. And so did Jolie. It would be the only way they could move forward.

A scuffing noise had him whirling. Cash stood in the doorway, a smirk on his face, thumbs hooked in his jeans' pockets, his expression nonchalant.

"I didn't figure you for a nostalgic fool, Cord."

His youngest brother resembled their father more and more every day, a thought that worried him. "What are you doing here, Cash?"

"I live here, too."

Cord just managed to stop the eye roll. "None of us live

here anymore. You and Chase have made a point of staying away, in fact."

"Some of us have jobs that keep us on the road."

"You didn't answer my question. Are you spying on me for the old man?"

Lifting one shoulder in a negligent shrug, Cash still wouldn't look directly at him. "Naw. Why bother?"

"But you just happened to wander up here." Yeah, right. Cord eyed his brother and didn't bother to hide his skepticism.

Cash stared at him. "The stairwell door was open." He stepped into the room and looked around. "Can't believe all this stuff is still here." He nudged one of the equipment bags with his foot.

"Miz Beth doesn't throw anything away, especially if it's even remotely sentimental." A lump formed in Cord's throat, and he swallowed around it to add, "Or had anything at all to do with one of us."

"Sentimental to who?" Cash delivered a savage kick to the bag.

"Her, I guess, since she pretty much raised us. She and Big John never missed any activity one of us was into. Clay's debates and speech tournaments. Chance's and my rodeos. All of our games from Mighty Mites Football and Little League until we were out of high school. I bet if we dig deep enough, the score books John kept are up here somewhere."

Cash's upper lip curled into a snarl. "Some of the kids thought they were our parents."

Cord stared at his brother, his gaze thoughtful as he considered where Cash's sudden vehemence came from. "At least they were there, bud. Our old man never made time for us in any way, shape or form." As Cord watched, an unidentified emotion flickered across Cash's face. It took a few moments for him to figure it out. "He wasn't there for us, either. None of us. He couldn't be bothered. Unless he was telling one of us what to do."

"Yeah, whatever." Cash kicked the bag again and then stared at him. "So what are you going to do about it?"

"About the old man?"

"No. About your own son."

Cord reached down and snagged a Tonka truck. CJ would like it. Tucking it under his arm, he brushed past Cash but paused at the door.

"I'm going to take care of him. Whatever it takes."

Seventeen

Jolie ignored the restaurant's bustle as she pushed the food on her plate around with her fork. She wasn't hungry—hadn't been since her blowup with Cord after Halloween. She'd somehow managed to get through Thanksgiving, but since then there'd been another fight about CJ's birthday. She'd refused to let him go with Cord, though she'd allowed Cord to talk to her son, and had given CJ the presents Cord dropped by. Despite her insistence she didn't want to talk to him, Cord called. Often. And like an idiot, she answered. He pushed to spend more and more time with CJ. And with her.

Christmas was two weeks away and her life was careening out of control. She didn't know how to avoid the train wreck. Glancing up, she found her father staring at her.

"He's not good enough for you."

She just barely resisted the urge to sigh. "Dad, please."

"You deserve better, Jolene. You deserve a man who will put you and CJ first. A man who will fight for you. Cordell Barron is not that man."

"People change."

"Not that much."

"You don't know him, Dad."

"I know him better than you do, baby girl."

She stared at her father, doing her best to decipher the expression on his face. There was more to all of this—

especially his bragging about knowing Cord well—than he was letting on. "What's that supposed to mean?"

He just looked enigmatic, cutting and eating his steak as though she hadn't asked the question. She seethed in silence, following his example. She'd watched him play this game all her life and she'd learned to play with the big boys. Using her father's tactics got her through college, and then through the admissions process for nursing school. Her clinicals. Her boards. And she'd used them when she insisted she was moving to Houston to have her baby.

"Why are you defending him?"

Opening her mouth to refute, she snapped her jaw shut before speaking. Her dad was right. She'd just defended Cord. The man she was mad at. The man who wanted to twist her world into Gordian knots. She'd had it up to her chinny-chin-chin with alpha men, including her father. But there was only one man who captured her thoughts, held them and made her do and say things totally against the grain. Cord Barron. Damn him.

A tense détente continued until Rand finished his dinner. She'd still barely touched hers. Her stomach roiled with tension. Their waitress cleared their plates, brought dessert Jolie hadn't ordered and filled her coffee cup. She added two creamers and an overflowing teaspoon of real sugar. Ignoring the crème brûlée, she sipped her coffee, watching her dad over the rim of the cup.

"Eat your dessert, Jolene. It's your favorite."

Huh. He'd broken the silence first. Interesting. She was even more curious about his motivation for this tête-à-tête dinner as a result. Indulging him, she spooned a bit of the creamy concoction.

"I'm not a little girl anymore, Dad. You can't divert my attention with treats." She laughed and almost choked. "Or ponies."

Rand chuckled at the memory. "Pony. Singular. And I'm not the one who decided to braid his tail with ribbons."

She smiled fondly, savored another creamy bite and then plastered a serious look on her face. "You should try being honest with me, Dad."

"I am, sugarplum."

"Ugh. First 'baby girl.' Now 'sugarplum.' 'Princess' can't be far behind. Good grief, Dad. When are you going to treat me like an adult?" She wagged her finger. "Do *not* tell me—" She inhaled, and in a reasonable facsimile of her father's voice said, "When you act like an adult."

"Jolene, you don't even know why he broke up with you."

"Want to bet?" She gloated a little over her father's expression. She'd certainly caught him off guard.

"Why don't you tell me the Barron version?"

So she did. She spoke of wanting Cord all through high school. She told him how she'd tried to seduce him at that ill-fated frat party and how Cord had been a perfect gentleman. She admitted to sneaking around behind everyone's backs.

"You were devastated when he broke up with you."

"Yeah, Dad, I was. I loved him. With my whole heart. I was nineteen and I'd given him my virginity." She didn't laugh when her dad blushed, and then stewed a little. "Jeez, Dad. I was, like, the only virgin in my graduating class. And that wasn't for a lack of trying on the boys' part. It's because none of those high school boys held a candle to Cordell Barron."

She finished off the custard and pushed the dish away. "He didn't tell me anything that night. He walked into my room, said, 'It's over' and walked right back out. When he found out about CJ, we talked. Cyrus Barron, that old bastard. Cord left me because his father didn't give him any choice."

"That's bull."

"No, Dad. It's not. You know that evil old man. He laid things out to Cord. Showed him what he could have right before jerking the rug out from under him. He was young. So was I."

Rand attempted to interrupt, but she held up a warning finger to stay him. "Let me finish. You asked what I know and believe. I'm telling you." She sipped her coffee and regrouped her thoughts, even though coffee wasn't what she wanted at the moment. What she really wanted was a good stiff drink. But she'd met her dad at the restaurant and was driving, so coffee would have to suffice.

"St. Paddy's Day. I was out with the girls celebrating passing our boards. And there he was at Hannigan's, with Cooper and some of the guys. I planned to seduce him, Dad. And then get up and walk away, leaving him like he left me. Only we were both so drunk birth control was the last thing on my mind."

She didn't get the rise she intended. Instead, he studied her for a long moment before speaking. "Interesting. That's pretty much the same story he told me when I asked him. Unusual for a man like him to admit a weakness."

Jolie didn't breathe for a moment and then sputtered, "You've talked to him?"

"I had a talk with him one day when I picked up CJ at the ranch." His gaze arrowed in on her. "What was his excuse for leaving you pregnant with my grandson?"

"That's all on me, Daddy." She scrubbed at her forehead with the heels of her hands, but the action did little to alleviate the headache blooming there. She couldn't meet his gaze for a long moment. "You know he didn't walk away when I was pregnant. I never told him."

Rand's expression never changed. Jolie caught no flicker of his thoughts revealed on his face or in his eyes. He simply stared, mouth grim, eyes half-hooded by his lids. When he finally spoke, his words tore at her nerves like a cheese grater.

"I raised you better than that. I didn't agree with you at the time, and look what's happened by keeping that secret."

He leaned back and folded his arms across his chest. "The boy might have surprised us both. I know the man has."

Before she could retort, her cell rang. She would have ignored it, but it was her home number. Jolie answered and Mrs. Corcoran's voice spilled out before she could even say hello.

"You have to come home. You have to come right now." The nanny's words ran together..

"Mrs. C? What's wrong?" Jumping to her feet, Jolie snatched her purse and jacket and headed for the exit. Rand tossed money on the table and followed at her heels. He didn't question her, but steered her to his car and handed her into the passenger seat. Jolie stayed on the phone, listening to Mrs. Corcoran. Fear prickled across her skin, with anger hot on its heels. Her voice tight with emotion, she kept up a running commentary so her father could catch up.

"It's CJ. Some men came to the door. They have papers. Mrs. C is too upset to make sense of them. They're taking CJ. One took him upstairs to get some clothes and his backpack. Mrs. C says he's terrified and crying." Then she put the call on speaker.

She shivered as her father reached across the console and patted her knee. "We'll get to the bottom of this."

Jolie knew he meant to reassure her, but it wasn't helping. What was going on? "Mrs. C? Mrs. C! I want to talk to whoever's in charge."

A man's voice cut through the nanny's hysteria. "This is Harris."

"This is Jolene Davis. Why are you at my house?"

"We have an emergency pickup order for the minor child, Cordell Joseph Davis, pending a hearing on termination of parental rights."

Her heart seized, and she couldn't force words past the pain in her chest. Her father took over.

"This is J. Rand Davis. You touch my grandson and I'll see your ass in jail."

"I have a court order, sir. We are removing the child per that order."

A wail tore from Jolie's very core, but she clapped hands over her mouth to cut it off as her dad squeezed her leg. "My daughter and I are en route. I'm also notifying my attorney. You will do nothing until we arrive."

"That's not the way it works." The line went dead.

Tears overflowed, and Jolie could barely breathe between the sobs, her fear and a boiling anger so strong she could melt the polar caps. By the time they arrived at her house, the men had gone, taking CJ with them. Mrs. Corcoran sat at the kitchen table, sobbing. A Nichols Hills police officer stood there looking uncertain. When Rand pressed for an explanation, the local cop explained that Mrs. Corcoran had hit the panic button on the security system's alarm panel and he'd responded, but not in time to stop the men.

"Yes, sir," he told Rand. "The papers are on the table. They were signed by a district judge. I'm sure sorry 'bout all this. Your nanny told me you were on your way, so I figured it best to stay here with her until you arrived."

"I appreciate that, Officer." Rand's voice left icicles in its wake.

Fifteen minutes later, Mrs. Corcoran had calmed enough to make coffee. Rand and Jolie had both read the papers the men left behind, but none of it made sense to her. When one of Rand's attorneys arrived, he quickly leafed through the papers and explained while Jolie paced the length of the family room, pivoted and paced back.

"CJ won't go into the foster care system. Judge Braxton signed the order, which appears to be civil, not criminal. The order was filed on behalf of the alleged father, and I'm guessing that's where they took your son."

"Have some coffee, honey." Mrs. Corcoran held out a mug as Jolie stalked past her.

Jolie didn't want coffee. She didn't want a drink. She wanted blood. If Cord Barron had been there, she would have sliced him into little pieces and fried him up with hash browns for breakfast. "That means Cord took him. He's probably at Cord's house right this minute. How do I get CJ back?"

The attorney continued perusing the paperwork and it was her father who answered. "I'll call Judge Wilson." Rand patted the seat next to him. "Sit down, Jolene, before you wear out the carpet. The judge owes me a favor. He'll sign a temporary order returning CJ to you."

She didn't want to sit, either. Anger surged through her veins, leaving her hot and cold in waves. "CJ must be scared to death, Daddy. I want him home." Jolie made another pass across the room. "I can't believe Cord would do this, the sorry son of a bitch."

Rand folded his arms across his chest. "I suspect he's gotten desperate, Jolene. You haven't exactly been trying to work through the custody issue with him."

"Whose side are you on, Dad?"

Mrs. Corcoran cleared her throat. "Miss Jolie? Wasn't CJ's daddy who came with those men."

Jolie stopped dead, fingers and toes tingling from the surge of adrenaline. "What do you mean, Mrs. C?"

"The man looked like Mr. Cord, but it wasn't him. When CJ saw him, the little tyke stopped cryin' and ran to him. Called him Uncle Cash."

"That's it." She grabbed her purse and coat. "Give me your keys, Daddy."

"What are you doing, Jolie?"

"I want my son back. I'm going to go get him."

When Rand didn't react fast enough, she rooted in the pockets of his overcoat, found the keys and dashed for the door. She didn't wait for the men as she jumped into her dad's SUV and headed off in a reckless charge to reclaim her little boy.

That twenty-minute drive was one of the longest in her life. As she parked in front of Cord's condo, she let her anger surge. By the time her dad and the attorney arrived, she was standing at the door, tight-lipped, hands fisted at her sides, her heart thudding. She was going to kill Cordell Barron for this.

She pounded on the door. "Cord, open up!" She pounded again and yelled even louder.

Lights blazed on inside and a voice yelled, "What the hell? I'm comin'. Give me a sec."

The locks on the door clicked and the door swung open to show a sleepy-eyed Cord with bed-tousled hair, wearing nothing but gray cotton gym shorts. He absently rubbed fingers through the hair on his chest as he blinked at her, and then registered the presence of her father and the attorney.

Jolie had a moment when anger and fear toppled over into arousal. Damn, but Cord was sexy. How could this man dissolve her into a puddle of wanton desire just by opening the door? Especially now, since, according to those papers, he'd taken her son. What was wrong with her?

Cord stared at Jolie, his eyes narrowing as he recognized J. Rand. The other man standing outside his door looked vaguely familiar, but he couldn't place him. "What the he—?"

His question was choked off as Jolie slapped him. "Where's CJ?"

Cord really regretted the beers he'd drunk with the pizza he'd ordered for dinner. Nothing was making sense—not the rude awakening, being slapped by Jolie or her question. Jolie looked frantic. And pissed. Very, very pissed. He wondered just how many beers he'd had to drink because he sure couldn't figure out what was happening. Before he could ask what she meant, she hit his chest with a balled-up fist. "Where is he? What have you done with him?"

Cord stared at her, wondering how a crazy woman could make his shorts tent. He backed up a step so she couldn't slug him again. He looked at the clock in the foyer. It was after midnight. He'd fallen asleep during the ten o'clock news. "What's going on, Jolie? Why are you asking about CJ?"

"You filed those papers you threatened me with. You're trying to take CJ away from me."

"I did what? Whoa, baby. Slow down, back up and re-wind. What papers?"

"You sent men to my house to get CJ. They had a…a…"

"A temporary custody order," the man who'd come in with Jolie and J. Rand finished. He stepped forward and gave Cord the evil eye. "Michael Weller. I'm representing Ms. Davis in this matter."

"What matter?" Cord figured he looked as confused as he felt. "Jolie, I have no idea what you're talking about. I haven't filed any papers. I don't know anything about a custody order, and I damn sure didn't send anyone to your house to get CJ. Are you saying some men took him? Where is he?"

"He's supposed to be here."

"Supposed to be *here*? Why? I'm telling you, he's not!" Panic threatened to close his trachea so he couldn't breathe, but he didn't have time for that. He had to find out what had happened to his son. "I didn't take him, Jolie." He half turned to Rand, but stopped as tears welled in Jolie's eyes. She looked so lost all he wanted to do was wrap her in his arms and make it all better. He reached for her, but she jerked up her shoulder in self-defense. "Baby, talk to me. What's going on? Where's CJ?" He reached for her again, and this time she fell into his arms, tears staining her cheeks.

"He's gone."

Eighteen

Heat drained from Cord's body, leaving only ice behind. "Who took him?"

"Your brother."

"Dammit, I have four brothers. Which one?" Cord attempted to focus, but his brain wasn't firing on all cylinders yet. Jolie's announcement had his heart racing like a hamster on a wheel. Who would take CJ? Chance? No way, not after what he and Cassie had gone through to be together. Chase wouldn't be bothered to leave Vegas. Or Nashville. Or wherever he currently happened to be. Clay was in Washington. He answered his own question when he ran out of brothers. "Cash."

She nodded mutely, trying to control her tears.

"I didn't have anything to do with this, Jolie. I promise we'll get him back." He breathed a little easier when her arms tightened around his waist. He brushed a kiss across the top of her head and reluctantly loosened his hold. "I need to get dressed and go get my—our son."

Jolie pushed away from him and flicked tangled hair back from her face. "I'm coming with you."

He didn't want Jolie there when he confronted Cash. Didn't want her to see how badly he'd been betrayed by his family, but he couldn't stop her, either. "I'll be ready in five minutes."

Four minutes later, he was locking the door and headed to his truck. Rand and Weller stood next to a Lexus, arguing with Jolie. She wheeled and marched toward him. "Where are we going?"

"The ranch."

She turned back to her father. "Do what you do best, Dad. I'll keep you posted." She climbed into his truck without help. Once they hit the interstate headed north, Cord barely spared her a glance as he focused on the lines on the highway, knuckles white where they gripped the steering wheel.

"Cord? Can we talk?"

"Not now, Jolie."

He'd never been so damn angry in his entire life. His old man had done some spectacularly stupid crap in his time. But this? Cord had no words—and any he might have wouldn't be coherent. The icy rage swirling in his gut left little room to think. Cord punched the Bluetooth button on the steering wheel and barked, "Call Chance."

Chance answered, sounding neither awake nor alert, which pissed Cord off for some reason. He yelled into the Bluetooth microphone, "Did you have anything to do with this?"

The sound of a jaw-snapping yawn echoed in the truck. "Do you know what time it is? What are you talking about, Cord?"

"Cash and some men showed up at Jolie's. They took CJ."

"Oh, hell, bud. What's our old man done now?"

"He filed some goddamned legal paper. Did you have anything to do with it, Chance?"

Stunned silence hummed in the truck, followed by bitter cussing streaming through the speaker. Cord had been thinking the same curse words. He swallowed and added, "I'm going to kill them, Chance. Both of them." He hit the end button and refused to answer when the screen lit up with an incoming call from Chance.

"You don't really mean that, Cord." Jolie sat twisted in

her seat so she could face him. She looked pale in the dim glow of dashboard lights.

"The hell I don't. That's my son, Jolie. *Our* son. You're his mother. They *took* him from you." He had to breathe around the burning knot in his chest before he could continue speaking, but then realized there was nothing else to say. He clamped his jaw shut and pressed the accelerator a little harder. The truck sped up and the white lines on the highway blurred beneath the big vehicle's tires.

At the ranch, Cord skidded to a stop in front of the main house, barreled out of the truck and sprinted for the front door. He didn't wait to see if Jolie was behind him. He hit the door with his booted foot and it crashed open. Miz Beth and Big John stood in the foyer. She was wringing her hands and John looked as if he was going to be sick.

"Where is he?"

"He's fine, Cord. He's asleep in his room." John's soft rumble attempted to convey a sense of calm, but he was as agitated as his wife.

Jolie's sobbing gasp kept Cord from storming up the stairs. He turned and pulled her to his chest, circling his arms around her shoulders. "Shh, baby. It's okay. We'll get him and go home."

"No. You won't." Cyrus stood in the arched doorway separating the entry from the great room. He glared at Jolie before flicking his gaze to Cord. "She's not welcome here."

"Fine. We'll get CJ and go."

The sound of screeching brakes outside sounded like nails on a blackboard. Cord didn't care. He just wanted to get CJ and go home with Jolie.

Cash stepped up to join his father and Cord saw red—literally. Before anyone could react, he strode to his brother and coldcocked him with a right hook to the jaw. Cash went down as if he'd been poleaxed. Cord turned to his father. "You're nothing but a dried-up piece of cow turd, old man.

I'm going upstairs to get my son, and then his mother and I are taking him home. I'm done with you."

"Cord—"

Chance was suddenly at his side. "Think, Cord. Just shut up and think."

Cyrus puffed up and opened his mouth but didn't get the chance to speak as both Cord and Chance rounded on him and said in tandem, "Shut up."

Cash began to stir. Chance offered him a hand up, which Cash ignored. He remained sitting, butt on the floor, knees bent, his forearms resting across them. He stared at Cord, surprise showing in his expression.

"When the hell did you learn to punch like that?"

"Shut up, Cash. I'm about two seconds from kicking the crap out of you." Cord looked around to apologize to Miz Beth, but realized she and Big John had disappeared. Jolie stood just inside the front door looking shell-shocked.

He faced his father. "What the hell were you thinkin', old man? Oh, wait. You weren't."

Cyrus bristled and jutted his chin, his expression as aggressive as the clenched fist he shook at Cord. "I'll tell you what I was thinkin', Cordell. And I'll tell you what I did. What you should have done months ago when that trash blew back into town with your bastard. I'm making sure my grandson grows up to be a Barron. A legitimate Barron. You should have given him your name—*our* name as soon as you found out. You should have made that boy yours."

The color red edged his vision again. If he didn't stroke out, he was going to beat his father to a bloody pulp. "You're wrong, Cyrus. He's not just my son. He's Jolie's, too. CJ will be a Barron. But he's also a Davis. CJ is our son. Jolie's and mine. I'm not taking him away from his mother. I want to share him with her."

Jolie stepped to his side and slipped her hand into his as Cyrus glared, his face a study in disappointment.

"I'm done with the lot of you. The boy stays here. He's

a Barron and he'll be raised as one. I'll make sure neither of you see him again. Take your whor—" Cyrus didn't get to finish the word as Cord's fist slammed into his jaw. He staggered back a half step before he straightened.

"You'll pay for this, Cordell. I will take away everything I ever gave you." His gaze brushed across Cash. "Clean this up, Cashion." With a final grunt meant to dismiss them all, he walked out the front door, his face a mask of disgust.

Cord shared a glance with Chance before staring down at his youngest brother. "You know, I thought it was pretty crappy when you had those foreclosure papers served on Cassie, but this? Damn, Cash. You are really rolling around the bottom of the outhouse now."

Cash wisely stayed on his butt. "Better me than a stranger, Cord. If the old man sent one of his thugs, we wouldn't know where CJ was. That's why *I* went to get him. And why I brought him here where—"

"What the—?" Cord forced his feet to take two steps back to put space between him and his brothers. "It would have been better not to do this at all. You could have stopped our old man. How could you do this to me? We're family."

Rather than kick—quite literally—his brother while he was down, Cord grabbed a decorative wooden box filled with doodads from a shelf and sent it crashing into the mirror hanging above a pine-and-deer-antler console table near the front door. The mirror shattered. "You're my goddamned brother, Cash, and you betrayed me."

Cash rolled to his feet in a lithe move. Without a glance at Cord or Chance, he strode to the door. He paused and stared back over his shoulder. "No, Cord. I'm not your goddamned brother. You and Chance and Clay are brothers. Chase and me? We never counted. We were always seconds." He walked out, slamming the door behind him, leaving Cord and Chance staring at each other.

Stunned, Cord found his voice first. "What was that

all about?" As he asked the mostly rhetorical question, he remembered his conversation with Cash in their old playroom. Yeah, the twins were technically half brothers to him, Chance and Clay, but he'd never considered them anything but family.

Chance frowned. "I don't know where that came from. We're brothers. All of us."

"Exactly. I always thought it was us against the old man. *All* of us, Chance. After the old man married Helen, she was our mom, the twins our brothers."

Tunneling his fingers through his hair, Cord felt rocked to his very foundation and completely out of control. He didn't like either feeling. At all. He wanted to grab the world with both hands and twist it, shape it, stuff it back into the mold he'd created so that everything was nice and neat and running the way he wanted it.

Chance stared at the closed door. "He's sure got a chip on his shoulder about something, though. I'll call Chase in the morning, see if he knows what's going on with Cash." Chance stepped closer and lowered his voice. "Look, we need to talk."

Cord sneered, but also replied in a quieter voice. "About Cash?"

"No. About—" Chance raised his hand in a vague wave "—all of this."

"Cash and a couple of his goons scared the nanny and took CJ. On the old man's orders. Without my knowledge or permission. What's there to talk about, Chance?" He held out his hand for Jolie. "Let's get CJ and go home."

Chance's next words pulled his attention back to his brother. "I want to see the order, check to see which judge signed it. This whole deal smells like an overflowing porta-potty on a hot July day."

"You got that right."

Chance exhaled and rubbed his eyes before addressing Jolie. "You may or may not believe me, Jolie, but here's the truth. Yes, I had a paternity test done to confirm that CJ is Cord's. And yes, I drew up some orders petitioning for a name change and amended birth certificate. Cord asked me to hold off filing. I did. I wish now I hadn't. If we'd fixed things in the beginning, it never would have come to this. I'm also positive that Cyrus used one of his pet legal sharks to draft whatever the hell was filed. I'm sorry. If you'll let me, I'd like to look at the paperwork you were given. And I'd like the opportunity to fix the mess my—" He choked off the expletive. "The mess our father made." He offered her a bitter smile. "Sadly, I've been there, done that and my wife occasionally sleeps in the T-shirt."

Jolie lifted a shoulder in a small shrug and flashed a tired smile. She leaned against Cord's arm as he gave her hand a gentle squeeze. "I'll go get CJ, 'kay?"

He nodded and reluctantly released her hand. Chance stepped up beside him as they watched Jolie climb the stairs. "We'll make this right, Cord. One way or another. And don't worry about the old man's threats. He can't do a thing. I've made sure he can't touch any of us."

Overcome with emotion, Cord grabbed his brother in a bear hug. "You've always had my back. You know I'll always have yours, right?"

Big John appeared with a broom and dustpan and cleared his throat. "Better get this mess swept up before the young 'un comes down."

Miz Beth arrived a moment later, dragging a large trash can behind her. Chance hurried to relieve her of it and bent to help John. The older woman touched Cord's arm. "Your father is a mean ole son of a gun, Cordell. Thank goodness you boys didn't fall close to that tree. I was ready to box Cash's ears when he walked in with CJ."

A quick laugh burst from Cord at the thought of tiny Miz Beth giving Cash what for. "At least he brought CJ here, Miz Beth, where you and Big John could look after him." And wasn't that what Cash had been trying to tell him? He'd been too pissed to listen.

Miz Beth used a corner of her apron to dash away the moisture gathered in her eyes. She was rising on her toes to plant a kiss on his cheek when Jolie screamed Cord's name. Miz Beth scrambled out of his way as he raced to the staircase and took the steps two at a time, Chance and Big John hard on his heels. He careened into CJ's room expecting to find blood-splattered walls or worse.

"Jolie? Jolie, baby. What's wrong?" Cord hauled her against his chest, checking out the room over her head. The bedclothes were rumpled but there was no sign of CJ. John checked the bathroom while Chance checked the closet and under the bed. CJ was nowhere to be found. John checked the window. It was closed and locked.

"Where is he, Cord?" Jolie seemed to clamp down on her panic. She gazed around the room. "Where's Ducky? Where's his backpack? Mrs. Corcoran said he'd had both with him when Cash took him."

"We'll search the house, Jolie. He can't be far."

"Do you... Would they...?" She was unable to finish her thought, but Cord knew what she was thinking.

"No. There's no way Cyrus or Cash could have taken him. He's here somewhere. Maybe he woke up and heard the yelling, got scared. He's probably hiding in the house."

They split up and searched the house from top to bottom, which took far longer than Cord wished. As they gathered downstairs in the kitchen, Big John appeared, a hangdog expression on his face. "Back door in the utility room isn't closed all the way. I'm sorry, Cord, but it looks as though he got out of the house." The older man glanced over his shoulder. "And it's starting to snow."

Nineteen

The weak winter sun poked at the clouds riding low on the eastern horizon and touched the light dusting of snow with a handful of sparkles. The serene scene did nothing to alleviate the tension in the kitchen. Dark shadows bruised the skin around Jolie's red-rimmed eyes. Her face was drawn and pale, and she looked as exhausted as Cord felt. Cassie sat next to her, attempting to get her to eat some of the eggs and bacon Miz Beth had cooked.

With Kaden's help, they'd searched the barn, all the farm equipment and the stables. They'd awakened the ranch hands and checked each of the cottages. There'd been no trace of CJ, nor had he answered their desperate shouts. They did discover that Dusty was missing, too. Cord tried to take some comfort in that. The dog was big and furry and hopefully keeping CJ warm overnight.

A local newscast droned in the background, and when the morning weather forecast came on, Big John turned up the volume. The prediction wasn't good. A big storm was due by noon, with plummeting temperatures and ice. They had to find CJ and find him now. Cord regretted calling off the search in the dark hours before dawn, but Chance, Kaden and Big John had all convinced him that stumbling around in the dark wasn't smart. With daylight, they could find tracks, follow them. And search teams would arrive.

The back door opened and heads swiveled, hope plastered on every face, only to be let down when Cash walked in. He held his hands at shoulder level, palms forward as if he was surrendering. "You may not want it, but I'm here to help, Cord." His gaze snapped to Jolie and he squared his shoulders. "I'm sorry, Jolie. This is my fault. I saw CJ at the top of the stairs last night, watching what was going on. I didn't say anything."

Cord made a fist, ready to take another swing at his younger brother when Chance's hand clamped on his shoulder. "Breathe, Cord. Last night is done. We need all the help we can get to find CJ before the storm hits."

Cord inhaled sharply, his gaze never leaving Cash's face until he heard Jolie move. He glanced at her and her eyes met his. She tucked her chin a bare inch, her expressive face filled with a rush of emotions. She broke their connection with a flick of her eyes toward Cash but returned to capture his gaze once more.

"Yes," she said, her eyes still boring into his, but her words meant for his brother. "It is your fault." Cash winced and stepped back. "You should have said something. You should have not taken him to begin with. I…" She balled up her fist and pounded the granite top of the breakfast bar.

Cord grabbed her hand, wrapped her up in a hug. He knew her frustration. He wanted to put his fist through a wall. Or his brother's face. Again. But Cash was here. Apologetic. Wanting to help.

"Jolie?" Rand called to her softly from the doorway. Cord was glad Jolie's father had finally arrived. He let her go and she ran to the other man. Rand patted her back and he murmured soft endearments to her, but his gaze remained first on Cord and then on Cash.

"I have a team with me, Cord, and two more on the way. If the weather clears, I can get at least two helicopters in the air. Hell, I'll put them up even if the weather doesn't." Cash still didn't step farther into the room. "Just tell me what you want, what you need."

Jolie pushed away from Rand and faced Cash. "You're

still a royal jerk, Cash, but thank you. We can use your help." She stepped toward Cord, and he closed the distance between them, sweeping her into his arms. "Bring him home, Cord. Bring our baby home."

Controlled chaos followed her plea. Cash opened the back door to usher in some of his security team. Cooper Tate and his brother, Bridger, tromped in carrying boxes of electronic gear. Cash waved them into the dining room. Deputies from the Logan County Sheriff's Office arrived, along with members of the volunteer fire department. The table that had been the scene of a family Thanksgiving just weeks ago now became their "war room."

Cassie watched the weather on TV while she helped Miz Beth make coffee and food. Jolie stood at the wide window overlooking the backyard. Cord appeared behind her and circled his arms around her middle. "We'll find him, Jolie."

"I'm scared, Cord. He's just a little boy."

"I know, baby. But us Barrons are stubborn cusses."

The strangled noise she made was either choked laughter or a sob. He stood with her, letting the babble from the dining room wash over him. When he heard doors opening, he hugged her, kissed the top of her head and disengaged. It was time to find CJ and bring him home. "I'll be back, sunshine. With our son."

He left her standing there. She looked frail, but looks were deceiving. She was one of the strongest women he knew. Words formed on the tip of his tongue, but he couldn't spit them out. Not yet. Not until CJ was safe. Then he'd tell her. He'd be able to say the words then.

The search teams had their assignments and spread out, going to work. Cord joined the team leaders on the front drive. He wanted to go, but Chance and Cash both overruled him.

"Stay with Jolie, Cord. She needs you. We'll find him." Chance's breath fogged the air until the brutal north wind shredded it. The temperature kept dropping, the sun a pallid circle behind thick clouds. His brothers pivoted and marched off to join their assigned teams.

Growls from ATVs drowned out shouts and excited barks from the search dogs. Close to fifty people milled around, getting sorted out, ready to do their jobs. Rand appeared at his shoulder and Cord spared him a glance. The older man looked as exhausted as Cord felt.

"I'm sorry, Rand."

"For what, son? You didn't make your daddy a jackass. And I probably should apologize to you. I knew about CJ. Knew he was yours. But Jolie—"

A wry chuckle escaped before Cord could cut it off. "Yeah. Jolie is a lot like her father. She wants to do things her way."

Rand slapped him on the back. "That she does, Cordell. That she does. Gonna take a special man to win and keep her."

"I'm workin' on that, sir. I surely am."

"Good."

The other man flipped up the collar of his coat and tilted his head toward the house. "It's colder than a two-dollar whore's heart out here. Let's get inside."

After the team leaders cleared out, Jolie returned to the kitchen and went through the motions of helping Miz Beth and Cassie. She needed to do something—*had* to do something to keep from going crazy. She mindlessly shoved cups and plates into the dishwasher, all the while listening to the radio traffic in the next room. The news wasn't good. The snow had come too late to show any tracks CJ might have left and the wind was playing havoc with the tracking dogs.

Where would CJ have gone? He'd only been out here to the ranch a few times—to swim in the heated pool, to ride horses in the corral, to play in the barn. He'd have told her if he had a special place out here. Wouldn't he? She dropped the coffee mug in her hand and ran into the other room. Cord wasn't there. Her father looked up, a question in his eyes.

"Where's Cord?"

He stepped into the room. "I'm here, Jolie. What's wrong?"

"CJ. Did he have a special place here?"

Cord's forehead furrowed in thought. "Like what? A hidey-hole? I mean, he has his room. He liked to play in the hayloft of the barn. The pool."

Her breath—and her enthusiasm—whooshed out in a sigh of disappointment. "Oh." She wrapped her arms across her chest to hide her shivers. "I just… I don't know. I thought maybe…"

"Maybe what?" Cord walked up to her, his expression grave.

"I thought there might be someplace he liked to go." She swiped her hair off her forehead and muttered, "Never mind," before retreating back to the kitchen. The babble in the dining room overwhelmed her. She couldn't understand all the radio messages, and trying to decipher them gave her a headache. Coffee. She'd get some coffee. Or maybe hot tea. She was numb, but cold leached into her very bones. As though it would rob her little boy of his heat, and maybe his life. A hard shiver stomped down her spine, kicking each one of her vertebrae until she just wanted to curl up in the fetal position.

"Hang on, baby. Hang on for Mommy."

Cord wanted to follow her, but the need to listen to the radio, to know exactly what was happening, held him frozen. He twisted around to look out the window, pressing his forehead against the cold glass. The gentle swells of the nearest pasture undulated like frozen waves. A dark line of trees loomed beyond the red barn. He stared but didn't see the snow-dusted landscape. Was Jolie on to something? She knew their little boy better than he did—at least for now. His mind replayed everything he and CJ had ever done here at the ranch.

They'd taken ATV rides. Fished in the lake. He quit breathing for a minute. Surely CJ wouldn't have gone to the lake, not when it was so cold outside. Whipping his head around, he yelled over to Bridger, who was working the radio communications. "The lake! Has anyone checked the lake?"

"First thing, Cord. There's no sign of him there. No tracks. And the mud wouldn't have frozen until this morning. The search party would see any prints if he'd gotten close to the water."

He breathed through the momentary panic. This wasn't helping. He felt sick inside. Looking up, he saw her in the doorway to the kitchen. She looked wrung out but he figured he didn't look much better.

"Miz Beth made tea. Do you want some?"

He walked over to her and gathered her into his arms. "Not thirsty, sunshine."

"I hate your father." Her words were muffled against his chest.

"Makes two of us."

"I'm sorry, Cord. For keeping CJ a secret. For fighting you. I've been so…scared. Of losing CJ because he might love you more than me."

"No, baby. That wouldn't happen. I want to be his dad. I want us to be a family. I don't want to take him away. Shh. S'okay. No more secrets, sunshine. Never again. Not between us." Her sob was also muffled in his shirt, but he felt the shudders racking through her. He held her, absorbed her fear and sorrow as she cried, and he shed a few tears of his own. He hadn't cried since his mother died. Or Helen, when she was killed by that drunk driver. The old man yelled when they cried. Called them weak. He had a place he'd run away to…

"Ah, crap!"

Jolie startled in his arms and he turned her loose. "Cord?"

"The caves. Why didn't I think of that?" If he'd been sitting at a desk he would have banged his head on it.

"Caves?"

"There are some caves in the hills down by the river. I used to go there. CJ and I rode out there one time. I told him about exploring them when I was a kid."

"Tell Bridger. Call one of the teams."

"The teams can't get to him. The terrain is too rugged for the ATVs. I'll have to ride."

"Ride?"

"Horseback. It's the quickest way to get there."

"I'm coming with you." She jutted her chin and her eyes flashed.

Cord dropped a soft kiss on her mouth. Seemed the Davis family was just as stubborn as the Barrons. "Put on warm clothes. Miz Beth will find some for you. I'll go saddle the horses."

They rode for twenty minutes, the north wind nipping and biting every inch of exposed flesh. Sleet pinged off their heavy coats and clung to the manes and hides of the horses. Even the animals seemed to be shivering despite their thick winter coats. They were ranch stock, bred to work. They weren't the hothouse purebloods Kaden used in the breeding program. They crossed terrain marked with steep arroyos with crumbling red dirt sides. They skirted rocky outcroppings and pushed through scrub brush thick enough that an ATV would have no chance. As they rode toward the river and the rocky hills where Cord's cave was located, he and Jolie took turns calling CJ's name.

He glanced over at her but couldn't see much of her face besides her eyes. He lowered his muffler. "Can I ask you something?"

Jolie turned her head to watch him. "I guess so?"

"Do you trust me?"

"What? Where'd that come from?"

"I need to know, Jolie. Do you trust me? With taking care of CJ? With taking care of…you?" She didn't answer and the wind kicked up again but he didn't pull the muffler up. "I need to know, baby. I need to know if there's any hope for us, and if you don't trust me, if you believe that I could do to our son—to you—what my father did…" He swallowed hard, choking back his anger. "Do you believe I'm like the old man?"

"Oh, God, no, Cord! You aren't like him."

"But…" He stared at her when she wouldn't look at him.

"Deep down, no, I didn't believe you would take CJ—not that way. But last night, when I got that call, I was scared. Terrified."

"So you don't trust me."

"That's not what I said." Real heat singed her voice. "Why are you asking me this stuff?"

"I need to know if we have a chance."

A bark echoed before she could reply. Cord stood up in his stirrups and let loose with a shrill whistle. Excited barking answered him. "Dusty!" He reined his horse around and headed toward a rocky hill at a canter. Jolie quickly caught up. Cord whistled again, and the barks sounded closer. A flash of black-and-white caught his eye. He pointed toward the dog racing their direction. "There! It *is* Dusty." He kicked his horse into a full gallop, Jolie's horse following.

They met the dog at the base of the hill, sliding their horses to a stop with a sharp pull on the reins. Cord swung out of the saddle with a grace born of practice and called Dusty to him. He ruffled the dog's ears and fur. "Where's CJ? Is he with you?" He studied the hillside, then cupped his hands and yelled, "CJ? Are you here?"

Jolie's voice joined in. "CJ? Mommy and Daddy are here! Where are you?"

"Mommy?" A thin, wavering voice floated down. "Daddy?"

Dusty barked and charged up the hill, Cord fast on his heels. "Stay there, Jolie. I'll bring him down. I promise."

Cord found CJ tucked back into a shallow cave, wrapped in a thin blanket. "C'mon, bubba. Time to go home." CJ leaped into his arms, and Cord simply held his son for a long moment.

CJ wrapped his arms around Cord's neck, his legs around his waist. With careful haste, aware of the terrain and prancing dog both waiting to trip him, Cord clamored down the hill. Jolie had dismounted, and she grabbed CJ from him, kissing and hugging the boy. Cord pulled the two-way radio from his saddle pack.

"Bridger, this is Cord. Can you read me?"

"Loud and clear, Cord."

"We have him." Cheers erupted on Bridger's end. "He's cold and hungry. We'll be back in about thirty."

"There will be an ambulance standing by. Safe trip, Cord. And good news, cuz!"

The doctors at Children's Hospital gave CJ a clean bill of health but wanted to keep him overnight for observation. Almost the entire family had trooped through, leaving stuffed animals, balloons and candy behind. When things finally calmed down, and Cord and Jolie were left alone in the hospital room, he asked the question Jolie had avoided thinking about since they'd found CJ.

"Why did you run away, CJ?"

"The yelling. It scared me."

Jolie clutched him to her and Cord wrapped his arms around them both. "I'm sorry, CJ. Sorry for everything."

"I didn't mean to be bad."

"Ah, CJ. Don't. You weren't bad. It wasn't your fault, bubba. Sometimes, grown-ups are just…dumb."

Jolie squeezed the little boy's hand, but her smile was

for Cord. "Yeah. Sometimes grown-ups are just dumb." She inhaled and blew the breath out hard enough to ruffle her bangs. "Yes."

Cord looked confused. "Yes?"

"Yes. I trust you. To take care of CJ. To take care of me. I trust you with my heart."

"Oh." A big goofy smile spread across his face. "Oh!" He scrambled off the bed and grabbed his coat. He dug in all the pockets, his expression growing more panicked. Searching in one last place, the inside left chest pocket that rode right over his heart, he found what he was looking for.

His big hand held something, but Jolie couldn't tell what. Her heart rate ratcheted up, and she tried to breathe around its pounding. He dropped to one knee beside the bed and she was vaguely aware that CJ clapped his hands and giggled. When Cord opened his hand, a black velvet box sat on his palm. Blood roared in her ears, and she gulped in a breath, reaching for a calm she didn't feel.

"Jolie, I love you. I think I fell in love the moment I first saw you. I've pretty much messed up from the very beginning, but if you'll give me a chance, I promise to love you and our son every day until there are no more days." He opened the box. A diamond-and-emerald ring glinted under the fluorescent hospital lights. "Jolene Renee Davis, will you do me the honor of being my wife? Of being the mother of my children? Of loving me even half as much as I love you?"

CJ poked her in the back. "Say yes, Mommy."

She blinked back tears, her cheeks aching from the smile that stretched them to the max. "Oh, yes, Cordell Thomas Barron. I will marry you." She fell into his arms. "I do love you. I love you with my whole heart."

Epilogue

Cord rolled over and gathered the woman sleeping at his side into his arms so they were spooned together. Jolie stirred and muttered something about sleep. He kissed her bare shoulder and rubbed his cheek against her sleep-tousled hair. Her lips looked plumped and she bore a slight rash from his beard stubble along her jawline. Considering this was their wedding day, he should feel bad about that, but didn't. That was what all the gunk littering the counter in the bathroom attached to the guest bedroom at Chance and Cassie's house was for. He cupped her breast, tracing his thumb over her nipple. It perked right up from his attention, but it was Jolie's grumbling that put a big grin on his face.

"I love you, sunshine."

She sighed, and he leaned over to capture the end of her breath with a gentle kiss. She shifted beneath him and he covered her with his body. If he were a gentleman, he'd go shower and shave before making love to her. But he wasn't. He was a man wildly in love with his woman, and he wanted to brand her as his for all time. Breaking their kiss, he trailed his lips down her chin and throat until he found her other breast. Flicking his tongue over that nipple, it caught up to its partner on the perky meter. She gasped as he scraped his teeth over the sensitive tip and his erection swelled.

Cord suckled her breast while his fingers continued to tease her other nipple. She arched beneath him, rubbing her thigh against him. He groaned and glanced at her. Eyes open, she watched him, her mouth quirked and her eyes narrowed. That was a dare if he'd ever seen one. With slow, sure certainty, he kissed his way across her rib cage. He paused at her belly button to lay a circle of kisses around its perimeter before dipping the tip of his tongue inside it. She giggled, as he knew she would. His Jolie was ticklish despite her protestations to the contrary.

Murmuring around the hitches in her breathing, she rolled her hips, tempting him to dip lower. He rubbed his chin through the soft curls at the juncture of her thighs. She opened farther for him. Well aware of the roughness of his morning stubble, he kissed her most secret of places—places he knew so well. He teased with his tongue and lips. And then he tasted her. Deeply. She was wet and ready for him.

"Please," she sighed.

"Please what, sunshine?"

"Please love me, Cord."

He rose above her and slid his aching erection into her softest depths. "Always, Jolie. I'll always love you."

He made slow, sweet love to her, their connection so deep he felt as if he was part of her—just as it should be. When he could stand it no longer, he shifted and angled her hips a little higher. Jolie's sharp inhalation told him he'd found the spot. Increasing the tempo, he drove them higher and higher until she clenched him and shuddered. His mouth crushed hers as his body followed her lead, and he swallowed his name on her lips.

Sometime later, Jolie cupped his cheeks and studied him. "Sweetheart?"

Cord crushed her to his chest. "I love you so damn much, Jolie. You're my life. You and CJ."

"You realize this is all kind of wrong, right? Making love on our wedding day, before the ceremony?" Her eyes twinkled and her mouth quirked in a mischievous smile.

"I'm going to start every day making love to the woman who branded my heart."

They had about thirty seconds' warning before a tiny whirlwind hit the door and blew through it. Cord managed to roll over and tuck Jolie into his side before CJ lunged onto the bed and started bouncing. "Mommy! Daddy! We're gettin' married today."

Laughing, he grabbed his son and pulled him down, careful to keep the blankets pulled over Jolie. Cord really needed to remember to lock their bedroom door. "We most definitely are, bubba. Go get Aunt Cassie to fix you breakfast. Mom and I will be down in a little bit."

"Okay!" Their son bestowed sloppy little-boy kisses on their cheeks, jumped off the bed and remembered to shut the door behind him.

Three hours later, the Crazy M ranch was filled with guests. Chance and Cassie had moved into the new house they'd built on her family property. Part luxurious log house and part historic Oklahoma giraffe rock, their home was a place of warmth and love—and the perfect place for Cord to marry Jolie. A large swath of early-spring grass carpeted an area between the house and a new barn. White chairs formed rows with a broad aisle down the middle—space wide enough for two horses to walk side by side.

Cord waited in the barn with his brothers. As they had for Chance the previous summer, they'd gathered in a show of solidarity. Chase had even turned off his cell phone. Cash was there as well, though he held himself apart from the rest. Cord would push Cash about his issues, but not today. Today was all about Jolie. And CJ. About becoming family. Horses snorted and pawed in their stalls, bridles jin-

gling. CJ bounced between his uncles. The horses had been
his idea. And the Western theme. Instead of tuxes, they
wore knife-edge pressed jeans. Cord's shirt was white, the
others' Oklahoma blue, and they all wore bolo ties cinched
with turquoise—his groomsmen gift to each of them.

When the time arrived, Cord helped CJ mount his horse.
The gray filly had been his Christmas gift to his son. He
mounted his chestnut quarter horse and his brothers followed suit. They rode out of the barn, single file. Kaden
waited at the back of the crowd to hold CJ's horse until it
was time for the boy to ride down the aisle. First, the men
would ride to the flower-entwined bentwood arbor where
the minister waited. The bridesmaids, also mounted, would
follow, then CJ, right before J. Rand escorted Jolie down
the aisle. In a rare show of humor, Kaden promised he
wouldn't let the bride bolt.

A local country band played a popular love song as his
brothers led the way. When Cord arrived, he dismounted
and turned to watch the procession. There were three
bridesmaids—friends of Jolie. Cassie, the matron of honor.
CJ. And then he saw Jolie. Soft sunshine painted the day
with pastel colors and cast a glow only surpassed by the
bride. He'd waited so long for this moment, hoped for it
with every fiber of his being, and there she was.

She reined her mare to a stop. Cord vaguely heard the
minister ask about who gave this woman. Then he was
moving to her, lifting her down from the horse, holding her
cradled in his arms before placing her on her feet. Words.
Music. More words. And then he had a ring in his hand, a
ring he slid on her finger as he said, "With this ring, I give
you my heart. On this day, I give my promise to walk with
you, hand in hand, wherever life takes us. I offer you my
heart, my soul. You and me. Together. Forever."

Jolie said the words back, slipping a ring on his finger.
Her eyes looked like emeralds sprinkled with diamonds,

just like the engagement ring he'd given her kneeling there in CJ's hospital room back in December. He felt back in control now, and all was right in his world as the minister pronounced them husband and wife and said he could kiss his bride. He did, whispering across her lips, "You are my sunshine."

* * * * *

If you loved
THE COWGIRL'S LITTLE SECRET
by Silver James
pick up the first book in her
RED DIRT ROYALTY series:

These Oklahoma millionaires work hard
and play harder.

COWGIRLS DON'T CRY

All available now from Harlequin Desire!

If you're on Twitter, tell us what you think of
Harlequin Desire! #harlequindesire

#2371 TRIPLE THE FUN
Billionaires and Babies • by Maureen Child

Nothing will stand between Connor and his triplets, not even their stubborn, sexy guardian. But Dina wants to raise the babies on her terms, even if it means resisting the most domineering—and desirable—man she's ever met.

#2372 MINDING HER BOSS'S BUSINESS
Dynasties: The Montoros • by Janice Maynard

Alex is on a royal mission for his country's throne. But when his assistant cozies up to a prince, unexpected jealously forces Alex to reevaluate his ideas about separating work from play...

#2373 KISSED BY A RANCHER
Lone Star Legends • by Sara Orwig

Josh seeks shelter at Abby's B&B...and gets snowed in! When they share a moonlit kiss, legend says it will lead to love. But can a cautious, small-town girl and a worldly Texas rancher turn myth into real romance?

#2374 THE SHEIKH'S PREGNANCY PROPOSAL
by Fiona Brand

After risking one passionate night with a sheikh, Sarah dismisses her dreams for a relationship—until her lover finds out she's pregnant. Suddenly, the rules change, because Gabe *must* marry the mother of his child!

#2375 SECRET HEIRESS, SECRET BABY
At Cain's Command • by Emily McKay

When Texas tycoon Grant Shepard seduced the lost Cain heiress, he ultimately walked away to protect her from her conniving family. But now she's back...and with a little secret that changes everything.

#2376 SEX, LIES AND THE CEO
Chicago Sons • by Barbara Dunlop

To prove the Colborns stole her late father's invention, Darci Rivers goes undercover at Colborn Aerospace—and even starts dating her billionaire boss! Can a double deception lead to an honest shot at happiness?

REQUEST YOUR FREE BOOKS!
2 FREE NOVELS PLUS 2 FREE GIFTS!

ALWAYS POWERFUL, PASSIONATE AND PROVOCATIVE

YES! Please send me 2 FREE Harlequin Desire® novels and my 2 FREE gifts (gifts are worth about $10). After receiving them, if I don't wish to receive any more books, I can return the shipping statement marked "cancel." If I don't cancel, I will receive 6 brand-new novels every month and be billed just $4.55 per book in the U.S. or $4.99 per book in Canada. That's a savings of at least 13% off the cover price! It's quite a bargain! Shipping and handling is just 50¢ per book in the U.S. and 75¢ per book in Canada.* I understand that accepting the 2 free books and gifts places me under no obligation to buy anything. I can always return a shipment and cancel at any time. Even if I never buy another book, the two free books and gifts are mine to keep forever.

225/326 HDN F4ZC

Name	(PLEASE PRINT)

Address	Apt. #

City	State/Prov.	Zip/Postal Code

Signature (if under 18, a parent or guardian must sign)

Mail to the Harlequin® Reader Service:
IN U.S.A.: P.O. Box 1867, Buffalo, NY 14240-1867
IN CANADA: P.O. Box 609, Fort Erie, Ontario L2A 5X3

Want to try two free books from another line?
Call 1-800-873-8635 or visit www.ReaderService.com.

* Terms and prices subject to change without notice. Prices do not include applicable taxes. Sales tax applicable in N.Y. Canadian residents will be charged applicable taxes. Offer not valid in Quebec. This offer is limited to one order per household. Not valid for current subscribers to Harlequin Desire books. All orders subject to credit approval. Credit or debit balances in a customer's account(s) may be offset by any other outstanding balance owed by or to the customer. Please allow 4 to 6 weeks for delivery. Offer available while quantities last.

Your Privacy—The Harlequin® Reader Service is committed to protecting your privacy. Our Privacy Policy is available online at www.ReaderService.com or upon request from the Harlequin Reader Service.

We make a portion of our mailing list available to reputable third parties that offer products we believe may interest you. If you prefer that we not exchange your name with third parties, or if you wish to clarify or modify your communication preferences, please visit us at www.ReaderService.com/consumerschoice or write to us at Harlequin Reader Service Preference Service, P.O. Box 9062, Buffalo, NY 14269. Include your complete name and address.

HD13R

THE WORLD IS BETTER WITH

Romance

Harlequin has everything from contemporary, passionate and heartwarming to suspenseful and inspirational stories.

Whatever your mood, we have a romance just for you!

Connect with us to find your next great read, special offers and more.